The Baker's Dozen

A NOVEL BY S.D. DENNY

ISBN-13: 978-0-9819631-1-2
Library of Congress Control Number: 2009901139

Publisher's Note

Peace In The Storm Publishing, LLC.
P.O. Box 1152
Pocono Summit, PA 18346
www.PeaceInTheStormPublishing.com

The Baker's Dozen

A NOVEL BY S.D. DENNY

Peace In The Storm Publishing, LLC

For my Father,
Philip Wayne Denny, Sr.
March 29, 1942 – March 6, 2009

I'll see you in the mountains…

Praise for The Baker's Dozen

"*The Baker's Dozen* will captivate you from page one. S.D. Denny has created a powerful page-turner!"

~ Elissa Gabrielle,
President & CEO,
Peace In The Storm Publishing

"*The Baker's Dozen* is an excellent debut novel. From the very beginning the story grabs you and has you sitting on the edge of your seat needing and wanting more!"

~OOSA Online Book Club

"S.D. Denny's intriguing writing style pulls her readers into the story, keeping them turning page after page to find out what's coming next in this family saga. Bree discovers that the perfect family she thought she had prior to her father's death was anything but perfect, and once the truth is disclosed, it's impossible to close this book until you've read the final word. *The Baker's Dozen* will leave readers talking about it's true to life characters long after the story's ending."

~Linda R. Herman, author of *Consequences*

"S.D. Denny brings to her writing just the right amount of passion and emotion to pull you in and will keep you turning pages well into the night! *The Baker's Dozen* delivers on every turn. Denny is definitely one of this author's favorites!"

~D.L. Sparks, author of *All That Glitters*

Acknowledgements

As I sit here basking in the joy of completing my first novel, I'm reminded of the very moment that the idea of *The Baker's Dozen* came to me. I wanted to write for some time, but stood still and waited for assurance. Suddenly, it hit me like a ton of bricks and it evolved from there. Writing this story has taken me on an unforgettable journey, and there were many who inspired and encouraged me in ways they'll never know.

First, I thank God for the gift and the mind to write and make a difference.

To my children: Thank you Vann, for turning down the music so I could think, and Robert, for putting basketball on hold while I took the time I needed to be creative. I love you both more than words could ever express.

Chrissy, thank you for showing me that for every cloud there *is* a silver lining. And to Davida for keeping me grounded with the constant reality checks! I love you both.

Ma, I thank you for having patience with me, even when I seemed to have lost my own. The unconditional love you continue to give your family is clearly God working through you and I know that you *will* be eternally blessed.

To my brother Tony and sisters Jackie, Jessie, Katie and Aimee - I thank you for all your love and support through thick and thin! I love you all.

To my nieces and nephews Cheyenne, Tyler, Alex, Camden, Ashyn, Christinee′, Alyvia and Jaxson – you make life so sweet and I thank you for that.

To all my aunts, uncles and cousins, too many to name, I thank each and every one of you for your excitement and support. Thank you for all your word of mouth advertising and street marketing! Big shout out to

Sabrina (I love you, girl) for everything you do! I can't explain the feeling I have in my heart when we're all together! Wish it never had to end…

Special thanks to my friends Lisa D, Barbara, Sam, Lisa T, Nancy, Yvette, Precious, Angie, Ebony, Patryce, Kim, my god sister, Kisha, Shannyn, Vee and so many more! You're all precious gems I found while traveling on this journey called *Life*.

Pam, I thank you for showering my father with your unselfish love until the end. We saw the rainbow and it hadn't even rained! That's peace…

And to my second mother, Auntie, I love you so much and will forever cherish you in my heart. Thank you for being you!

Thank you, Chanel! I knew you'd see my vision and design the perfect cover and website. Visit Chanel and Web Presence Designs at www.w-p-d.net.

Big shouts go out to Elissa Gabrielle and the Peace in the Storm Publishing family! Thank you so much for believing in me and encouraging me to share my voice. I invite everyone to stop by www.peaceinthestormpublishing.com to see the fine collection of authors and books that are available! And to my friends at Authors Supporting Authors (ASA), thank you for always encouraging, networking and sharing your gifts. Visit www.freewebs.com/asanetwork for a real treat!

My father said he always knew I'd be a writer and although he's no longer here, I thank him for the difference he made in my life and for believing in me until the end.

Finally, I thank everyone who took the time to read *The Baker's Dozen*. I hope you were as moved after reading it as I was after writing it. Please share your comments with me at sddenny2003@yahoo.com or visit me at www.sddenny.com.

Never Underestimate The Power of Passion!

ONE

I'll never forget the look on Daddy's face as he lay limp and lifeless at the bottom of the stairs. His eyes were open and fixed on the front door, looking as though he'd seen a ghost. Mama was on her knees next to him crying, while Deanna was crouched against the railing at the top of the stairs peering through two wooden slats with tears streaming down her face. He'd been drinking and had fallen from the top, breaking his neck as he hit the bottom. Mama and Dee witnessed everything while everyone else slept. I woke up and ran out of my room when I heard screaming, but it was too late; Daddy was already dead.

I cried quietly in the shower as my thoughts led back to that horrible night fourteen years ago. Before the accident I led a carefree life. At least it didn't seem as harsh. Afterwards, I'd grown cold and learned how to suppress my feelings and pretend like nothing fazed me. Sometimes I wished I were the same person I was years ago, but life has a way of transforming you and since I couldn't change what had happened, I learned to adapt to people and things around me. After the accident, Mama seemed distant most of the time and my twin sister, Deanna, just shut herself down completely. Eventually, she went to live with our grandparents because they could dedicate more time to caring for her. The rest of my eleven siblings and I handled things as best we could with what we had to work with. It seemed unfair, but I learned to play with the hand I'd been dealt.

I stood in the shower with hot water beating against my neck and back, clutching my abdomen to see if it felt different. The news of my pregnancy was shocking and seemed like the beginning of a horrible nightmare.

Lord, why me? This can't be happening again. I was careful. This should never have happened. I can't handle this – that's all to it! And I can't tell Charles.

"Bree!" Charles yelled from the bedroom. "What are you doing in there? Did you fall asleep?"

I straightened up and rinsed the tears away, while managing to let out a sluggish reply.

"I'll be out in a minute."

As I stepped out of the shower I caught a hint of frying bacon and flew over to the toilet, gagging from the greasy stench. Normally, I loved that smell, but for the last couple of weeks I'd apparently been suffering from morning sickness, the second sign I'd gotten that something was wrong. After missing my period, I knew I was in trouble. I'd given my period a week to show up in the event something else may have been wrong, but to my dismay, it never came. That's when I decided to call Dr. McGhee for an appointment. I was *not* ready for the news I received yesterday that I was five weeks pregnant with Charles' baby.

Grabbing a towel on my way down, I knelt in front of the commode and threw up for the next five minutes. Charles invited himself in to check on me and I'm sure the last thing he expected to see was me on the floor throwing up.

"What's wrong, baby?" he asked. "I heard you in here gagging and I called, but you didn't answer."

He reached for my arm to help me get off my knees.

"I'll be alright. I must've eaten something that didn't agree with me last night. My stomach's been in knots since Camilla and I left the restaurant."

I'd never had a reason to lie to Charles and it made me uneasy. I'd called him from work and told him that we were working late and would grab a bite to eat before heading home. I needed to share the news of my pregnancy with my best friend.

"What in the world did you eat?" Charles asked as he patted my back with a towel.

"Just a burger, but you know I like them cooked medium and maybe the meat had already gone bad."

I cringed as I walked past Charles back into the bedroom. I hated the thought of being deceptive to him.

"I suppose you won't be joining me for breakfast this morning then?"

Charles looked disappointed as he sat down on the bed. We'd already established a breakfast tradition, just like my family had when I was growing up. Every day before heading our separate ways, we'd sit at the kitchen table and eat breakfast together. It was our little checkpoint of the day to make sure we were both on the same page.

"I'm sorry, baby. I just don't think my stomach can handle any food right now."

Charles reached for my hand and slowly pulled me down on his lap. He loosened the plush towel I had wrapped around me and it fell to the floor, revealing my naked body. He kissed my neck and made his way down to my breast, and the hairs stood on my arms as I grew more aroused. I never *could* resist his touch. I melted in his strong arms whenever they were wrapped around me. This tall, dark, and very handsome man was conveniently at my daily disposal, and truth be told, I was in love with him.

"Bree. Bree!"

His voice echoed into my thoughts and I came back to reality.

"Yes, baby?" I said with my eyes still closed.

"Maybe you won't mind if I have *you* for breakfast." He moved the hair from over my eye. "You're so beautiful, baby."

Often, before we made love, Charles would play with my hair, which I normally wore just past my shoulders. He always said it felt so silky between his fingers and it turned him on. And when we showered together, he'd just stand there and stare at me while the water ran through my hair and over my shoulders. He loved to watch the beads of water glisten against my pecan tanned skin.

Charles lifted my petite frame and laid me on my back on the edge of our bed. He made love to me, and as usual, it was magical – as though he read my thoughts and knew exactly where to touch me and what to do to please me. We connected as though we were made for each other.

"Charles, we're going to be late," I said, noticing the time.

We jumped into the shower together to save time, but Charles couldn't keep his hands to himself. I gave him a playful nudge in his side to make him hurry so that I'd have enough time to do my hair and makeup.

"It feels different," Charles said, rinsing the soap off my back.

"What feels different, baby?"

"Making love to you. It's like the feeling I have when I am inside you has intensified or something. I can't put my finger on it, but it's like I just can't get enough."

"Nah, you're just going through a horny stage or something, that's all."

We laughed and I changed the subject. I wanted to stay far away from any conversations about my body changing. I did not want him to know that I'd gotten pregnant. I wasn't exactly sure how he would react to the news. There was always the possibility that he'd want to get married and I surely was not ready for that. On the other hand, maybe he was not ready for a baby either. I couldn't know for sure unless I told him and I wasn't taking any chances.

Five months ago, Charles brought up the idea of marriage for the first time after we'd been dating for a year, but I convinced him to hold off. I suggested that we move in together first, just to see how things would work out before making a permanent commitment. Surprisingly he agreed, but with the stipulation that we'd talk about marriage again after six months. It was final; we found a cozy apartment and moved in together. We've successfully co-existed for five months, and I *would* have to pop up pregnant now! I don't think he'd agree if I told him I planned to terminate the pregnancy, so to keep things simple, I just wouldn't tell him. I could decide on my own. Besides, it's my body and that made it my choice. I loved Charles, and if there were such a thing as forever, he'd be the one I'd want to spend it with, but in my world forever doesn't exist.

I hurried to do my hair and makeup, and when Charles and I were both dressed, we grabbed our laptops, kissed each other, and were off to work.

TWO

Camilla pulled into the parking lot just as I exited my apartment building. We decided that it made sense for us to carpool in weekly shifts since we both lived in Marietta and worked for the same company in Atlanta. We've been best friends since elementary school back home in Charlotte. She came to Georgia to attend Clark Atlanta University after graduating from high school, and after receiving her Bachelor's Degree in Business Administration, she landed a management level job offer at an operations center for a large bank. I stayed in Charlotte, trying to help Mama with my younger sisters and brothers, while working and attending the University of North Carolina. I also graduated with a degree in Business Administration, but because I had to work to help out with bills, it took me a few years longer than it had taken Camilla to graduate. About a year after I'd graduated, Camilla called to tell me of a management level job opening in the training and development department where she worked. She felt confident that I would do a great job in the position, and with her recommendation, I had a greater chance of being offered the job. Within a week, I'd flown to Atlanta for an interview and a week later they called and made an offer. It was exciting and scary all at the same time. I'd dedicated my life to helping Mama hold things together after Daddy died, and the thought of leaving her made me feel guilty, but she insisted that I accept the offer. She knew I had dreams of being independent one day and she didn't want to hold me back from experiencing all the things that life had to offer.

"Spread your wings, baby," is what Mama always said when I talked about what I'd do after graduating college.

I knew it would be difficult for Mama to see me leave, and I knew that it would be just as difficult for me. Nevertheless, I called to inform the company that I'd accepted their offer and within a month, I'd moved to Atlanta. I stayed with Camilla for a few months while I worked and saved enough money to get my own place and buy furniture. Since she and I were so close, I had a hard time adjusting when Camilla went away to college, but there we were back together again, both thirty years old and still single. I didn't know what I'd do without her.

As Camilla pulled closer to the curb, I opened the passenger door and slid in. I sat my briefcase on the floor under my legs and rested my purse in my lap.

"Good morning," I said as I fixed my hair in the mirror on the visor, tucking a long lock behind my ear.

"Good morning back," Camilla said, looking at me as though she were waiting for me to tell her something.

"Well, did you tell Charles yet?"

"No, I *told* you that I can't go through with this right now. And if I tell Charles, there's no way he's going to agree with what I'm planning."

"Bree, how are you gonna look Charles in his eye afterwards? I don't think you can do it. And furthermore…"

"Camilla, please. What Charles doesn't know won't hurt him," I said, cutting her off in mid sentence.

"You don't really believe that. And I wish you would at least take some time to think about it. Don't make any rash decisions. That's all I have to say."

"Thank you," I said, giving her the evil eye.

The ride in to work had turned quiet and all the way in, I thought about the look on Dr. McGhee's face when she gave me the results of my pregnancy test. I also thought about the love that Charles and I had made this morning, and then my thoughts turned to Mama and my brothers and sisters back home. I'd been so wrapped up in work lately that I hadn't been home in about six months. We'd been working on a project that involved changing over to a new computer system for the entire operations center, and I'd been doing so much training that I'd hardly thought about anything else.

After arriving at work, we made our way to the break room to grab some coffee.

"So, we'll finish that conversation at lunch, right? I think I'm in the mood for some barbecue. How do ribs sound?"

Camilla raised an eyebrow as she waited for my reply.

"I've said all I have to say, Camilla, but ribs sound great," I said.

"See you at one o' clock sharp in the parking lot, Scrooge," Camilla said as she picked up her briefcase, rolled her eyes, and took off in the other direction.

I smiled and watched her sashay out of the break room with the ease of a runway model. Camilla was only five-foot-six, but her lean, fit frame made her appear taller. She always wore perfectly tailored clothing in the latest fashions that flowed right along with her, complimenting her manicured nails and fresh, short tapered haircut. She was the picture of flawless beauty and always made sure that her appearance was above average. I couldn't help but admire Camilla, even when I thought she was being unreasonable.

I grabbed my things and headed toward the opposite end of the building. When I got to my office, I immediately started my daily routine. Every morning I'd unpack my laptop and start it up, check the phone for voicemails that may have come in, and then check my email in the event there were any issues that needed my attention before I'd begin working. Finally, I'd check my calendar and task list for the day to see what meetings I had on my schedule and projects that needed prioritizing.

Great! No meetings until this afternoon. I need some time with no interruptions to work on this training plan.

I spent the remainder of the morning working on my training plan and before I knew it, it was almost time to meet Camilla for lunch. I grabbed my purse and headed for the ladies room to freshen up. After stopping for a brief moment to update my manager on my progress with the training plan, I headed for the parking lot to meet Camilla. She had already gotten the car and pulled up to the curb. Camilla had put on her sunglasses and was blasting the stereo. I slid into the passenger seat and turned to Camilla, grimacing as she bounced in her seat to the beat.

"You can take the girl outta the ghetto, but you can't take the ghetto outta the girl." I just shook my head and sighed.

Although Camilla didn't actually grow up in the ghetto, she didn't have a problem hanging out there. That was one of the things I loved most about her; she didn't discriminate even though her mother tended to be a little more *bougie*. Camilla and I lived in the same average neighborhood and attended the same schools until she moved away around the time we went to middle school. She was an only child, and after her parents divorced, her mother sold their house and they moved to a ritzy apartment community on the north side of town because she didn't want the responsibility of maintaining a home alone. By that time, Camilla and I had become best friends and had stayed in touch after she moved. I often spent weekends with her after Daddy died and Dee went away. It seemed that the closeness I shared with Dee was replaced by my friendship with Camilla, which grew into a sisterhood that I treasured as much as the relationship I once had with my twin sister.

I got in the car and Camilla pulled out of the parking lot, headed toward The Rib Cage, where they had the best barbecued ribs, potato salad, and coleslaw in town. It was always busy at lunch time, but they had fast and friendly service. After we'd eaten and had refills of iced tea, I caught our server's attention and asked for the check. Whenever I didn't have to drive, I'd treat Camilla to lunch that week.

As I stood to leave, Camilla grabbed my hand and looked at me with sadness in her eyes.

"Bree, I want to talk to you about something."

"Camilla, if this is about me being pregnant, I just…"

She cut me off in mid sentence.

"Bree, please just listen to me. You know I love you like a sister. You and I couldn't be any closer if we *were* sisters and all I want for you is the best. You have that in Charles, and I want you to give this some more thought before doing anything that you might regret later on."

I put my hand on top of hers and gave it a gentle squeeze.

"Camilla, I *have* given this some thought. And I've made my decision. I'm not…"

"You can't keep living in the past, Bree," Camilla cut in.

At that moment, she struck a nerve and something inside of me snapped.

"Camilla, I am *not* living in the past! I need you to understand, if I'm not ready, I'm just not ready. '

"Girl, when are you gonna understand that you can't be prepared for everything that life sends your way? Every move you make can't be some strategically calculated decision. It's just like in boxing – they have to roll with the punches because they don't always know if it's coming from the left or the right."

The look on my face told Camilla that I didn't want to continue with this discussion. I had nothing else to say on the subject and even though she made a lot of sense, I had to deal with this matter my way.

"We'd better head back to work," I said, looking away from Camilla as I rose and headed toward the door.

You could hear a pin drop in the silence as we rode back to work. Camilla had turned down the volume on the stereo as though she hoped I'd pick up where she left off in our conversation at the restaurant. I wasn't about to travel down that road again, so I pretended to search through the CDs in her collection until we got closer to work. I hurried to get out of the car in the parking lot, and told Camilla that I had to hurry back to prepare for a three o' clock conference call that I planned to facilitate.

As soon as I got back to my office, I opened my laptop and dug right into finalizing the training plan. Glancing over at the phone on my desk, I noticed the red light blinking, indicating that I had voice messages. I'd become so engulfed in my work that I hadn't noticed it when I first sat down. Eager to see who called, I punched in the code to retrieve my messages.

Two new messages.

The first was from Stacey Allen, one of the regional Training Managers, asking if I would add something to the agenda for today's meeting. I quickly pulled up the Word document, added her agenda item, and clicked *Save*. The second message was from Charles.

"Hey, baby. Hope your day is going well. You had me feeling so good this morning that I forgot to tell you that your mother called when you were in the shower. She asked me to tell you to call her as soon as you got the message. She said it's important. Sorry this message is late. Love you, baby. Bye."

Damn!

I was a little angry that Charles gave me this message so late, but I guess it was better late than never. I picked up the phone to call Mama. She answered on the second ring and I turned on the speaker so I could go shut the door to my office and talk in private.

"Hey, Mama. I got your message."

"Hi, Bree. It's only been eight hours since I called," Mama said sarcastically.

With my back leaning against the door, I thought of a quick response.

"I'm sorry, Mama. I've been preparing for an important meeting and it slipped my mind that you called. Is everything okay?"

I thought it would be better take the wrap for calling so late rather than put the blame on Charles. I didn't want Mama to have any reason to dislike him.

"I'm sorry to tell you this, Bree, but Granny passed away this morning. Papa called and said she went in her sleep. I just got back home from seeing him. He's okay – your Aunt Geri was with him when I left."

Mama kept talking, but she started sounding far away and the room got darker. The next thing I knew, I was on the floor of my office and Camilla was on her knees fanning me while a few of my co-workers watched with whispered.

"We heard a loud noise in your office and when we opened the door, you were on the floor and your mother was on the speakerphone calling your name," Jacqueline said. She sat in the cubicle right outside my office.

"Okay everyone; let's give Breanna some breathing room."

Camilla, although she was much thinner, had no problem as she helped me up from the floor and into a chair. After ushering everyone out of my office, she closed the door and opened a bottle of water for me. I took a few slow sips.

"Bree, your mother was still on the phone when Jacqueline came into your office. She told Jacqueline about your grandmother passing away and Jacqueline called my extension. I'm so sorry."

"Yeah, things suddenly started sounding far away and the room started spinning. The next thing I saw was you on the floor next to me."

"Do you want me to call Charles?"

"No, please. I don't want him to know I passed out."

"Well, I don't have anything pressing on my plate for the rest of the afternoon, so I'll take you home, okay?"

"Thanks, Camilla."

We stopped at my manager's office on the way out and gave her the agenda so that she could facilitate the meeting on my behalf. She told me not to worry and to take all the time off that I needed. Apparently, Camilla had already informed her of the news about my grandmother and everything had been taken care of, so we headed to Camilla's office to get her things and left.

I felt relieved to finally arrive at my apartment. Camilla came up to make sure that I made it in safely and to fix me some tea. Before she left, I promised her that I would call her later this evening when I felt like talking, and then I locked the door behind her. I couldn't call Mama back right now – I just needed to deal with the news about Granny, so I lay on the bed and cried myself to sleep.

THREE

The noise from Charles coming in from work awakened me from a three hour nap. It took me by surprise that he'd come home so early. As supervisor of one of the larger departments of a mortgage collection agency in Atlanta, he liked to stay after most of his employees' shifts have ended so he could run reports and get ready for the next day.

"Bree, what are you doing in bed so early?" Charles looked just as surprised to see me.

"I came home early today. Granny passed away in her sleep this morning. That's what Mama called to tell me."

My voice turned shaky and my eyes swelled with tears. When I couldn't hold back any longer, the tears started flowing. Charles came over to the bed and held me in his arms, wiping my tears away with his fingers.

"Oh, baby! I'm so sorry. I know how much Granny meant to you. Are you gonna be alright?"

"Yeah, I'll be okay. It's just that she was the only grandmother I had left, and I'm gonna miss her so much."

I buried my face in Charles' shoulder and cried while he rocked me in his arms for a while longer. After I'd gathered my composure, he offered to fix dinner.

"You have to eat something," he said as he went into the kitchen and fixed two Caesar salads topped with croutons, bacon, and grilled chicken.

I decided to call Mama back to see if any arrangements had been made yet for Granny's funeral. There shouldn't be too much confusion since there weren't too many opinions to get in the way. Granny and Papa only had two children, Daddy and Aunt Geraldine, who we call Aunt Geri for short. She and Uncle Bill and their adopted daughter, Sonetta, live in Fort Mill, South Carolina, a small town right outside of Charlotte, right down the street from Granny and Papa. And it's a good thing that they did because I'd hate to see Papa have to go through this all alone. He and Granny just celebrated their fifty-fifth wedding anniversary last year. That's a long time to be with someone and suddenly they're gone. Just the thought of what Papa might be going through made my heart ache. I've got to call him, but most of all, I've got to get to Charlotte to see about my family.

Mama said that Papa and Aunt Geri settled on Saturday for the funeral. We talked for nearly an hour about Papa and she updated me on my brothers and sisters. She told me about my oldest brother, BJ's promotion at UPS, where he'd been working since he graduated from high school. Daddy helped my two oldest brothers, BJ and Kory, to get jobs at UPS right after finishing high school. He said he didn't want his boys on the street getting into trouble, and because he'd worked there as a truck driver for many years, Daddy had a lot of influence with his supervisors. BJ was now thirty-three and still working at UPS. He'd made a career out of it, starting as a driver and working his way up to becoming a Supervisor. However, Kory, who was now thirty-one, was much more passionate about being an auto mechanic and left a few years ago to start a business of his own.

She also said that my brother, Dante, who was next to the last child to be born, had done really well in school this year and had one more year to go before graduating from my alma mater, UNCC. He's been studying computer science and was looking forward to landing a job with Microsoft after he graduated. It seemed as though everyone was doing okay, but Mama sounded worried about my baby sister, Bliss. She just graduated from high school and Mama wanted her to consider going to college, but Bliss told her she'd rather get a job and start making money right away so she could move out on her own. Mama also said that she thought Bliss might be dancing in a night club. She's been staying out late on weekends and having large amounts of money that she couldn't explain. I told Mama that I'd be home some time the next day and that I'd look into things with Bliss when I got there.

After dinner, Charles and I sat at the table with our planners and discussed the trip. I decided I'd leave tomorrow morning after breakfast and since Charlotte was only four hours away, I'd drive my car. Charles said he'd fly to Charlotte on Friday evening after work, and then we'd drive back together on Sunday afternoon. I liked the idea of having a couple of days alone to spend with my family. And I couldn't wait to see Papa and Aunt Geri. Although this was a sad occasion, I think seeing my family was just what I needed right now.

I packed my bags before going to bed so that I could take off right after breakfast. I'd forgotten to call Camilla back after dinner, so I gave her a quick call to let her know that I would be leaving for Charlotte first thing in the morning.

"Call me when you get there, Bree. Don't forget."

"Thanks for being there when I need you, Camilla."

"That's what sisters do. Just consider yourself the sister I never had," she said. "So we'll talk tomorrow afternoon, okay?"

"Okay, good night."

Camilla wasn't outwardly affectionate. She didn't have any siblings or many family members, and never really spent time caring for anyone but herself, with the exception of me, of course.

After I'd showered and gotten into bed, Charles reached over, pulled me closer to him, and held me. Before long, we were wrapped in each other's arms making love. We'd surely miss each other for the next three days, and we held each other as though it were our last time together. Afterwards, I fell asleep in his arms, dreaming of my sister Deanna and Papa.

FOUR

I awakened to the sound of Charles showering and birds singing outside our window. Even if I *wanted* to sleep in, the noise made it impossible. Forcing myself out of bed, I went over to the window and took a peek at the thrashers wrestling in the shrubs below, thinking how funny it would be if we mated like them. At least *they* don't have all the emotional baggage we have.

"Good morning! What can I get you for breakfast?"

My attention turned to Charles who was standing outside our bathroom drying off from his shower. The birds had me so intrigued that I hadn't heard him get out.

"Just a bagel is fine. I have to get on the road."

"Sounds good. Are you all packed?"

"Yep. I got everything done last night. I just have to shower and I'll be ready."

"Okay, well why don't you go ahead and jump in and I'll fix breakfast. Coffee sound good?"

"Sure, coffee's fine. I need something to help perk me up."

I breezed past Charles, giving him a peck on the forehead as he bent over to dry his legs and feet.

"See you in a few."

The steamy warmth from Charles' shower still filled the bathroom, so I hurried to shut the door before the cool air could creep in. As I stepped into thc shower, I thought about how accommodating Charles had been since I received the news about Granny yesterday.

I knew the night I met him that I'd stumbled across a rare gem. Camilla had coerced me once again to go with her to a monthly networking mixer at the downtown Hilton. All I really wanted to do on Fridays after a long week was go home, get into something comfortable, and ball up on the sofa with something good to eat and a good movie. But, she wouldn't give up until I gave in, so we headed downtown after work.

We went straight to the bar for drinks when we arrived, and I did as usual – stood there and watched people while my best friend, the social butterfly, worked the room. This time, Camilla made her way back over to me sooner than I'd expected.

"Bree, don't look right now, but there's a cute guy directly behind me sitting at a table all by himself and he's checking you out."

I peeked over her shoulder.

"Didn't I tell you not to look right now?" she said with her teeth clenched. "He's going to know I'm talking about him."

Camilla turned around as though she were looking for someone.

"Oh, my goodness! Bree, he's coming this way. Talk to him." Camilla took a sip of scotch and walked away as though she'd suddenly found the person she was looking for.

I continued to stare into the crowd, pretending not to see him coming.

He got the bartender's attention. "French Connection," he said.

He looked at me and smiled. "How are you tonight?" he asked.

"I'm fine, and you?" I replied, partially smiling back.

"I'm good, thanks." He paused. "My name is Charles."

"Nice to meet you, Charles. I'm Breanna."

"So, what brings you here tonight, Breanna?" he asked, taking the first sip from his drink.

"Actually, my best friend twisted my arm. I'd normally be home curled up with a good movie. What about you?" I asked.

Charles laughed. "One of my colleagues has been trying to get me to go out for weeks. I finally gave in and told him I'd meet him here tonight, but I haven't seen him yet."

The conversation took off from there. We eventually found a table where we sat and talked for what seemed like forever. I learned that he was originally from Savannah, but had relocated to Atlanta with his job a few years ago.

Charles was a true southern gentleman from the start. When he revealed that he was single and had no children, I was floored.

"I find it hard to believe that a man like you isn't attached at the hip to *someone*."

"A man like me?" he asked. "What about you? I'm just waiting for some man to walk over here and ask what's going on." Charles laughed and took another sip.

I found myself extremely attracted to him from the start. He was much taller than me – about six-foot-two with an average build. He had the smoothest cocoa colored skin and dreamiest brown eyes, and I loved how he wore his hair cut close. I wasn't too big on facial hair and was glad that he only wore a goatee instead of a full beard. But my attraction to Charles wasn't just physical; he also possessed certain "down home" qualities that made him stand out from the average, good-looking guys I'd met around here. I could tell he came from good people who instilled good values in him at a young age.

"Tell me about your family," I said.

"Well, Mom and Dad are still together and live in Savannah. They both work for the Savannah school system. I also have a younger sister, Tiffany, who's *also* an educator. I had to be the one to break the tradition."

I laughed. "It's okay. I'm not a big traditionalist, myself."

"So, are you free tomorrow night, Breanna?"

"Excuse me? Are you asking me out?"

"Well, you *did* say you like movies, right? How about dinner and a movie?" he asked.

I was flattered. "Alright. What time?" I asked.

"I can pick you up at six and we'll play the rest by ear. How's that?

Just as we had exchanged numbers, Camilla approached our table.

"There you two are. Listen, I hate to break up the party, but it's getting late. Breanna, are you riding with me tonight?"

I grabbed my purse. "Charles, it was nice meeting you. I had a good time."

"It was my pleasure, Breanna." He stood and reached for my hand. "So, I'll see you tomorrow then?"

Camilla looked puzzled.

"Yes. I'm looking forward to it." I shook his hand and we left.

"So, you're seeing him tomorrow?" Camilla looked pleased. "You haven't been out on a date in ages."

She was right. It *had* been a while since I've been out on a date, but I was sick and tired of meeting guys who just wanted to be friends with benefits. And, they didn't mind telling you. I didn't want to sell myself short, so I buried myself in my work and only thought about men from time to time when the urge to be close to someone came over me and even then I suppressed it by overworking myself.

"Yes. He asked me out to dinner and a movie."

"Wow! I think I like what's-his-name already."

"His name is Charles and you don't even know him," I said.

"No, but there's something different about him. I've got a good feeling about this one, Bree."

Camilla was right. There *was* something different about Charles. We'd ended up seeing each other again on Sunday and every weekend since then, and here we are almost one and a half years later, still together. After I'd met his family and he met mine, everyone gave their approval and we became an item. We have a good thing between the two of us, so why do anything to mess that up. Like the saying goes, "*If it ain't broke don't fix it.*"

"Breanna," Charles peeked into the bathroom, "your bagel and coffee are ready."

"I'll be right out," I replied as I finished rinsing the soap away.

When I came out of the shower with the towel wrapped around me, Charles stood behind me and cleared the fog from the mirror over the bathroom sink. He rested his chin on top of my head and stared at me for a few seconds.

"You're beautiful, baby," he said.

"Thank you," I replied, reaching for my toothbrush.

Charles ran his finger around the edge of my towel and I grabbed his hand.

"Didn't you just tell me that my bagel was ready?"

"What? Aren't you going to miss me, Bree?" He smiled.

"We can certainly make it through three days being apart," I teased.

"You *kill* me trying to be so nonchalant," he said. "You just don't know how much that turns me on."

"You're sick," I replied.

Charles laughed. "I'm going to the kitchen if you care to join me for breakfast before you leave."

"I'll be there in a couple minutes," I said, sticking the tooth brush in my mouth.

When I was done, Charles and I ate breakfast and headed back into the bedroom to finish getting dressed. We decided to pull out together, so when he was ready for work, he carried my bags to the car while I carried his laptop and we loaded up.

"Don't stop at any deserted rest areas and in the event of an emergency, don't accept any rides with strangers. Keep your door locked and call me as soon as you get to Charlotte." Charles had all kinds of precautionary advice for me.

"Okay. Okay. I know the routine." I put my arms around his neck and gave him a long kiss before getting into my car.

"Fasten your seatbelt," he said. "I love you and I'll see you Friday."

"Love you, too. See you Friday." And I was off.

FIVE

After struggling through an hour of stopping and going in the thick Atlanta rush hour traffic, I finally began making headway on the four hour drive up I-85 North. When I'd gotten outside the city limits and saw the countryside all around me, I set the cruise control to seventy miles per hour, slid a jazz CD into the player, and positioned myself comfortably in my seat for the ride I had ahead of me.

The trip home to Charlotte wasn't long at all; I just hadn't been home in over six months because I'd been focusing on work. With deadlines nearing, back to back meetings, and departments that remained untrained on the organization's new computer system, I never considered taking a vacation. In fact, I believe I've either gone into the office or worked at home every Saturday for the past three or four months, helping with system testing. It felt good to get away from the office, but I never dreamed it would be for this purpose.

Just then, I passed a tall tree on the side of the road covered in Kudzu vine and shaped like a person holding a serving tray. I immediately thought of Granny and how she would cook big dinners every Sunday because she knew we'd be coming to spend the afternoon. Laughing children surrounded the table filled with hot, steamy soul food as they reached for biscuits and were slapped on the hand for eating before saying grace. Those were the moments my brothers and sisters and I lived for, but things changed after Daddy died. My older brothers began finding other things to take up their time on Sundays; they either had girlfriends who they went to see, or they'd work on their cars and were too busy to enjoy Sunday dinner with family.

"Bring us a plate," they'd holler as we pulled out of the driveway headed to Granny and Papa's house, which was about a fifteen minute drive to the suburban town of Fort Mill in South Carolina.

Eventually, as we all got older, our family visits to Granny and Papa's house stopped. I rather enjoyed the time away from home, so I continued to make it a point to visit them every Sunday, even if it meant going alone. Granny never stopped cooking her Sunday dinners and there were always plenty of leftovers, so I took extras home for everyone. Granny and Papa loved to see me pulling up in their driveway, and whenever I left they'd stand in the doorway until I pulled out onto the road, then the porch light would go out and they were off to bed to relax and watch television. They were lucky to have each other to love for so many years. I know that Papa would never be the same after losing her; neither will I, but I have to be strong enough to help him get through these next few days. I had to hold it together so that we could give Granny a beautiful home going service. That's what she would want.

Taking a deep breath, I reached into the glove compartment for the pile of napkins that I'd collected on my fast food visits. I needed to change the tone of this drive, so I wiped the tears from my face and repositioned myself upright in my seat. The jazz CD added to my overflow of emotions, so I flipped open the CD wallet and searched for something more upbeat.

I came across an old mix CD near the back of the wallet that I hadn't heard in a while, so I popped it in the player and sat upright in my seat. The very first track took me back to my college partying days and I couldn't help but smile as I bobbed my head to the beat. I heard this song the night I met my ex-boyfriend, Linden, for the first time. He'd come to Charlotte to hang out for the weekend with a couple of his friends from UNC Chapel Hill, where he lived on campus and attended law school. I'd been hanging out with a couple of my co-workers and we ended up at the same club. Linden and I were attracted to each other from the start and after a couple drinks and a dance that ended up lasting nearly an hour, we exchanged phone numbers. The next day, we met at the lake near the university where we walked and talked for hours. We were obviously feeling each other and before we said goodbye that day, we'd already mapped out the next time we'd see each other. I planned to drive to Chapel Hill the following weekend for a Tar Heel game, and even though I wasn't a big football fan, we used it as an opportunity to see each other again and spend some time getting to know each other. It was also the first of many weekend drives we'd make in the whirlwind romance that shaped my opinion of love and relationships for years to come.

It's been years since Linden and I ended our relationship, but I still think of him from time to time and wonder how he's doing. He came to Charlotte after he finished school and worked as an attorney for an uptown firm, but I hadn't seen or heard from him since I left Charlotte a few years ago. The possibility of seeing him while I was home never crossed my mind before now, but surely after he heard about Granny, he'd show up to pay his last respects at her funeral. Somehow, my heart smiled at the thought of seeing him again.

For the rest of the drive, I thought about my family in Charlotte. I reminisced about the fun we had growing up in such a large family. Mama and Daddy had twelve children, which was something you just don't see too often these days. Some of their friends teased us and called us "The Baker's Dozen." I suppose my parents had a good marriage; they had lots of offspring to show for it. They dated their junior and senior years in high school and got married right after graduation, starting a family immediately. Daddy said that Mama was as beautiful as the sunrise, but was quite shy so he had to break through several layers to finally get next to her. She had very fair skin and long hair, and people thought she was mixed, but Mama said both her parents, who passed away when we were very young, were also very fair skinned and it just ran in the family. Mama, who was a twin herself, ended up having three sets of twins and six single births. There were eight girls and four boys starting with the oldest, Barnett, Jr. who was now thirty-three years old and ending with the youngest, Bliss, who just turned eighteen. And surprisingly enough, we all ended up with the same fair skin tone that had been passed down throughout Mama's entire family.

My parents did a great job taking care of the twelve of us. Daddy made a good living working at UPS, and he also owned a dump truck and contracted his services out to a few companies to make more money. Mama, on the other hand, was a stay at home mom. There was no way she could work with so many children to take care of, so she relied on her cooking and crafty skills for extra money to help out with the bills where she could to buy things that Daddy sometimes thought were unnecessary. She baked and sold her famous pies and cakes around town and also did a lot of sewing and alteration work for people in the neighborhood and at church. Mama was such a good seamstress that she started making wedding dresses for people. Word of mouth advertising got her a great deal of business, and she did well enough financially to use her money toward other things while Daddy paid the mortgage and took care of the major bills in the house.

We lived in a five bedroom, two-story house in a mixed neighborhood on a side of town that was once considered affluent, but over time the neighborhood had become just average. Noise always filled our house with so many kids running around. Even while most of us slept at night, someone always stirred around. Daddy worked at UPS and did most of his driving at night, so when he came home after work he'd sit up and watch late night television while having a beer. Mama, on the other hand, would sleep through the night from the exhaustion of baking, sewing, and caring for twelve kids all day. Just to get us all ready for school and out of the house on time to catch the school bus took a lot of energy. She'd make sure we had something quick to eat for breakfast every morning, and always had something ready to be stuffed into our lunch bags before we rushed out the door to catch the bus.

With all the rushing that went on in my house, I always looked forward to the weekends. On Saturday mornings we got the chance to sleep late, and on Sunday mornings Mama always made a big, hot breakfast. Usually, everyone gathered at the breakfast table by nine o'clock, ready for the spread that Mama would lay out in her signature buffet style. She always found ways to be creative with cooking, entertaining, and decorating.

After breakfast on Sundays, some of us went to church with Mama. Most of the boys begged Daddy if they could stay at home with him because they couldn't tolerate the length of the service, and even though Mama didn't like the idea, Daddy wasn't big on going to church so he agreed to let them skip it. On the other hand, I looked forward to going to church with Mama. Some of my sisters and I were members of the youth choir and very active in the congregation, so we were never bored. Mama had attended the same church while growing up and we continued the tradition, so the church members were like family to us.

For most of my childhood, I'd been surrounded by either my real family or my church family, so I never really felt alone, especially considering how close my twin sister and I were. Deanna and I did everything together. One of us rarely went anywhere without the other. They say that twins can feel each others' emotions and I can attest to that. Whenever Dee was unhappy, I could sense it and things weren't right with me until she was okay, and vice versa. And I could always count on her to be on my side, whether I was right or wrong. We were like two bodies sharing one soul, and not having her around made me feel as though a part of me had died. That's why Camilla and I became so close after Deanna went to live with Granny and Papa. Our friendship grew and we became attached at the hip as though it had always been that way.

Without thinking, I picked up my cell phone and started typing Camilla's name until the list of her contact numbers appeared on the screen. Scrolling down, I selected "Office" and waited for her answer. I started to think she might be away from her desk, but she finally answered on the third ring.

"Hey, Bree! You already in Charlotte?" Camilla asked, looking at her caller ID.

"No. Not yet. I've already passed through Spartanburg, so I'll be there in another forty-five minutes or so. How's work?"

"Everything's good. I heard your training plan went over well on the conference call yesterday, and I'm having a quick check-in with the managers after lunch today to see where they all are with their task lists. Don't worry, Bree. I'll make sure nothing falls through the cracks."

"I know you will, Mill. Am I gonna see you for the services Saturday?"

"Of course. I loved her like she was my own grandmother! I'm flying in Friday after work. My mother's picking me up. I'll call you when I get there."

"Alright. I'll talk to you then."

"Bree, we need to talk when you get back," Camilla whispered as though she were hiding a secret.

"Okay, bye."

"Bree, don't act like you didn't hear me. We need to talk."

"I said okay. I'm coming up on some traffic, so I have to go."

"Alright. Bye," Camilla mumbled in frustration before hanging up.

I had to find a way to get her off the phone before she started up again on the conversation we had over lunch yesterday. Camilla didn't give up when she was trying to make a point, but I was just as stubborn, so when we have a difference of opinion about something, it's like we're both fighting a losing battle. Eventually, we'd both retreat to our corners, throw in the towel, and move on.

I smiled and shook my head as I checked my surroundings to see how far I'd gotten and how much further I had to go. I noticed the sign saying Exit 90 in Gaffney, South Carolina and saw the Prime Outlets to my left. I knew it would be another thirty to forty-five minutes before I'd be home. I couldn't wait to see the sign saying I-485, which meant I'd be home in a matter of minutes. I sat back and savored the idea of home for the remainder of my ride.

SIX

Mama had just pulled into the driveway as I turned the corner to our street. I pulled in directly behind her, grabbed my purse, and ran to meet her.

"Bree! I didn't know what time you were gonna get in," she said, reaching out to hug me.

"Hey, Mama! You okay? You look tired." We shared a long embrace.

I noticed that Mama was beginning to look older. She still looked good for a fifty-one year old woman, but time and hard work was beginning to take its toll on her and it showed on her face and in the number of gray hairs on her head.

"I'm fine. You almost missed me. I *was* on my way to Granny and Papa's house to take some food, but I forgot the potato salad, so I came back for it. People are going to start dropping by and I want to make sure there's plenty of food," Mama said, heading toward the front door. "You need some help with your bags?" she asked.

"I've got 'em," I replied, grabbing my bags from the back seat of the car.

Once inside, I headed upstairs to the bedroom that Dee and I shared growing up. My younger sister, Monica, currently occupied it after moving out of the room that she shared with her twin, Veronica. My youngest sister, Bliss, had the room at the end of the hall, right next door to Mama's. The room hadn't changed much, aside from the fact that there were now two beds instead of three. On the bed at the far side of the room, there were two monogrammed throws that Mama made for Dee and me when we were kids. They were neatly folded and hung over the footboard. I lay my garment bag on the bed, sat the duffle bag and the laptop on the floor, and ran back downstairs to the kitchen where Mama struggled trying to fit the bowl of potato salad into a plastic bag.

"Where is everyone?" I asked, grabbing the bag to help her.

"The twins and Dante are at work and Bliss is just "o-u-t" as she calls it." Mama looked frustrated.

"BJ, Kory, and everyone else should be stopping by whenever they get a chance."

Mama tightened the lid on the bowl of potato salad.

"Oh, Bree, before I forget…" she handed me a sticky note with a name and number on it.

"Linden called? When?" I asked, looking surprised.

"He called this morning. He said he saw Kory after work yesterday and heard about Granny. When I told him you were on your way home, he asked me to take down his number and give it to you. He wants you to call him sometime today." Mama peered over the rim of her glasses with raised eyebrows.

"I'll call him this evening," I said, tucking the sticky note into the side zipper of my purse.

"So, what are we taking to Granny and Papa's?" I asked, changing the subject.

"I fried some chicken, and made some potato salad and a pound cake. I know I'm getting old because I totally forgot the salad. Good thing I wasn't too far away when I thought about it."

"You ready to go?" I asked.

"I'm so glad you're home, Bree," Mama said, smiling as we headed out the door.

We transferred the food from Mama's car to mine and were on our way to see Papa. The smell of the fried chicken reminded me of Granny's Sunday dinners and I couldn't wait to get to the house just to be around her things. I decided I'd take the back road down Highway 160 to give Mama and me some time to talk.

"So how's Charles doing and when is he going to get here?" Mama asked.

"He's good. And he's catching a flight after work Friday evening. We're gonna drive back together on Sunday," I replied.

"But I wanna know about Granny. What happened, Mama?" I asked.

"She just went in her sleep, Bree. They said it wasn't a heart attack or anything particular they could find. Her heart just stopped beating," Mama replied as she rested her hand on top of mine against the gear shift.

"What's gonna happen to Papa and Dee?"

"Papa's a strong seventy-four year-old man and he's able to take care of himself. We just have to make sure he's alright in his heart, because he's gonna miss

Granny. They were married fifty-five years, you know – ever since they were eighteen years old."

"And Dee?" I asked.

"She's been with Papa and Granny so long, it's her home. Time will tell if we need to make any changes, but for now I think everything's fine with Dee staying right where she is," Mama replied.

We continued on the rest of our drive to South Carolina in silence. I thought about the comment Mama made about Papa being strong in his old age and I remembered the story Granny told me about how he worked in the textile mill in Fort Mill since they got married when they were eighteen. Papa worked there until he retired almost ten years ago. He wasn't bad in the kitchen either, so we don't have to worry about him going hungry and with Aunt Geri right down the road, we knew that he and Dee would be alright.

"So, anything new with Aunt Geri?" I asked, trying to brighten the mood.

"Not that I know of. She still has her home day care and Uncle Bill still works at the car dealership. Wait 'till you see Sonetta. She's gotten taller with her pretty self. She's gonna be fourteen in August, you know."

Aunt Geri, short for Geraldine, was Daddy's older sister. She and Uncle Bill loved children but never had any, so they decided to adopt and were very happy when Sonetta came along. In fact, Aunt Geri loved children so much she started a home day care and have been caring for kids ever since.

"Time sure flies. Seems like just last year she was a baby," I mumbled.

"Bree, don't miss your turn." Mama pointed ahead.

I don't know what I was thinking," I said, slowing the car to turn right after passing the peach orchards.

A few minutes later, I turned onto Old Orchard Road. The smell of freshly cut grass was the first thing I noticed, and as I got closer to the house, I could see Papa on his riding lawn mower in the front yard. My head was flooded with memories of the summer days my brothers and sisters and I ran down the road past Aunt Geri's house to the dead end to pick peaches. Granny would make peach cobbler for us to eat with Papa's homemade ice cream. The last time I came home, it was winter and I didn't have the fresh grass smell or the fruit trees to remind me of the summer days we spent in Fort Mill when we were young.

Papa turned when he heard my car approaching. When he noticed who I was, he began making his way over to the edge of the yard closest to the driveway and parked the mower. He wore his favorite denim overalls over a white undershirt and work boots. He hadn't changed a bit since I last saw him. His head was still full of pure white hair, which looked so distinguished on his creamy brown complexion. Papa stood about six feet with a muscular build, and when he smiled, those pearly whites were the first things you'd see. As attractive as he was, Granny was even more beautiful with shoulder length, silvery hair that topped her glowing face, and she also had a smile that lit up the room. She was a petite, but quite feisty woman and Papa would tease her and call her Big Mama when she became angry. I could just imagine how disappointed the young ladies were to find that he only had eyes for Granny when they were teenagers. It must have broken many hearts to see the announcement of their engagement in the local newspaper: **Barnett Baker and Beulah Mae Owens to Wed.** Those poor women had no choice but to eat their hearts out because if ever there was a match made in heaven, it was Barnett and Beulah Mae Baker hands down.

"Bree! When did you get home?" Papa asked with excitement as he shut off the engine to the mower.

"I just got here, Papa! I came right over to see you," I replied, running toward him with outstretched arms, ready to hug him tight.

Papa and I hugged for a few moments. I can't quite pinpoint when it started, but tears were streaming down my face.

"I miss her so much already. I know you miss her, too."

"I miss her, too, Bree. Lord knows it's not gonna be easy, but we have to find a way to go on living. That's what she would want us to do."

Papa took a step back, looked me over, and took a handkerchief out of his pocket to wipe my tears away.

"Look at you! You get more and more beautiful every time I see you. Got a *special* glow about you today," Papa remarked, totally changing the subject as he dabbed at my cheeks.

I wondered what he could have meant by a *special* glow. Surely he couldn't see right through me to the secret I was hiding.

"Hello, Mayva. Whatcha got there?" he asked, walking over to give Mama a hand with the bags.

"Fried chicken, potato salad, and a pound cake. Now this ain't for you to eat in one sitting, Papa!" she said jokingly.

"Let's take the food inside."

We followed Papa into the side door that led to the kitchen. As I walked into the kitchen, goose bumps stood up on my arms and neck. Granny's presence was very strong and just looking around the intimate setting of her favorite place to be besides Papa's arms caused an emotional eruption in my heart.

"So, what's going on at that job of yours, Bree?" Papa asked, placing the bowl of salad in the refrigerator and everything else on the counter.

"Well, we're getting ready to make some big changes, which have taken a lot of planning and training, so that's why you haven't seen me in about six months. I've been putting in a lot of hours at work trying to prepare. I'm sorry I wasn't here, Papa," I said, grabbing his hands as he sat across the table from Mama and me.

"Is there anything you need me to do while I'm here? I can help clean up or…"

"Not much cleaning to do. I'm home all day, so the house is in order. But I *could* use your help going through some of your Granny's important papers. Might need you to run an errand or two also if you don't mind," Papa said as he cleaned the dust from his eyeglasses.

"I'm gonna get the papers out this afternoon. Maybe this evening you after you've spent some time with your mother you can come back over and we can go through 'em together. How does that sound?" Papa asked.

"Sure, Papa. We'll eat dinner together," I replied.

"I'll come back around seven," I added.

"Okay. Why don't you go see your sister, she's in the room watching television."

I gave him a wink and headed down the hall to the back room that he built onto the house years ago for Deanna. The door was opened wide enough for me to see Dee rocking back and forth in her favorite chair, half facing the window and half facing the television. The curtains were open and the sun shone brightly through the window, overlooking the freshly mowed back yard.

Deanna watched CNN, which she'd preferred to watch all day ever since she came to live with Papa and Granny from the Care Center. She'd gone to live at the Care Center when she was almost seventeen, and had stayed there for four years going through a program that helped minors suffering from mental disorders brought on by trauma. Dee suffered severe shock after witnessing Daddy's accident. They say she was traumatized so badly that she never recovered. They did all they could at the Care Center, and later released her to the care of Granny and Papa when she turned twenty-one. She's been here with them ever since.

"Hey, Dee!" I said enthusiastically as I placed my hand on her shoulder.

Dee stopped rocking and without looking at me, she reached up and placed her hand on top of mine. I kissed her forehead and found a spot on the floor in front of her.

"I've missed you, Dee. I've been working crazy hours, so I haven't been able to get home in a little while. I got the news about Granny yesterday and came home as soon as I could. We're all gonna miss her so much." I paused as though I were waiting for a response.

Dee just stared out of the window, not responding at all. I knew she wouldn't, but sometimes a glimmer of hope caused me to wish she'd just say one word. It's as though she no longer had a soul.

"Anyway, I'll be home for a few days so we can spend some time together. I'm coming back over tonight and I might even sleep over. Would you like that?"

She didn't reply.

As I stood to leave, I noticed her hair looked a bit matted as if she hadn't brushed it in days.

"I'll make your hair look nice and pretty when I get back. Okay?"

Dee's eyes followed me toward the door as I left, but she didn't speak a word. I knew that she was glad to see me by the warmth that I felt as she caressed my hand when I touched her.

Maybe tonight we'll have more of a connection.

I looked forward to getting back later to spend time with Papa and Dee. Walking back to the kitchen, I suddenly remembered that I hadn't called Charles and Camilla to tell them that I'd arrived in Charlotte.

"Ready to head back, Bree?" Mama asked, placing her half-finished glass of iced tea in the sink.

"Yep," I responded quickly.

I grabbed my purse and hugged Papa again, assuring him that I'd be back later so we could have dinner together before going through Granny's papers. Papa went back to tending to his yard work as Mama and I pulled out of the driveway heading back to Charlotte. With hunger beginning to set in, I looked forward to getting back so I could have lunch and grab a nap. Normally, I'd be wide awake this time of day, but suddenly I became overwhelmed by the need to sleep and I realized it must be the pregnancy. Everything seems to be changing.

SEVEN

Back at the house, Mama and I feasted on some leftover homemade vegetable soup she had in the fridge, while we talked more about the things going on in my brothers' and sisters' lives since I'd last been home. Bliss' new gig as a club dancer upset her most of all. I assured Mama that I'd talk to her and make sure things weren't getting out of hand, and perhaps even try to talk her into going to college. But right now sleep was calling my name and I had no choice but to answer.

"Mama, I'm a little tired from the drive. I think I'm gonna take a little nap."

I got up and cleared the table, while Mama cleaned up in the kitchen and headed upstairs. I had to call Charles and Camilla to let them know that I made it home safely. Sliding the garment bag over on the bed, I sat down and dialed Charles' cell phone number.

"Hey, Bree!" Charles sounded relieved to hear my voice.

"Are you there yet? I started to worry when I hadn't heard from you."

"I'm sorry. I got here about an hour ago and we went to take some food over to Papa's. How's everything going at work?"

"Work is good, but I'm gonna miss my little mama at home. How's your grandfather holding up?"

"Exceptionally well, considering the circumstances. I'm going back over there this evening to spend the night with him and Dee. Just call my cell phone if you need me."

"Alright, baby. I'm about to run out and get some lunch, so I'll talk to you later."

"Bye," I replied, keeping it short. I felt exhausted and had one more call to make before taking a nap. Barely able to keep my eyes open, I dialed the digits to Camilla's cell phone and got her voice mail.

"Mill, I'm in Charlotte. I got here around noon and just got back from seeing Papa. I'm tired, so I'm gonna take a nap. I'll call you when I get a chance. Bye."

Sleep couldn't come soon enough and before long I snuggled up with my old monogrammed throw, staring out of the bedroom window into the sky. I wondered what Linden and I would talk about if I called him and what it would be like seeing him again.

The sting from the pain and disappointment of how he chose his career over me was still very fresh in my mind. I remembered it just like it was yesterday. Linden was nearly finished school when I became pregnant, and all the love he claimed to have for me wasn't enough to make up for putting his career on hold if he'd become a father at that time. Not to mention the disappointment he'd have to face from his snooty parents in Long Island about fathering a child at that time in his life. So, I let Linden talk me into terminating the pregnancy, thinking it was the best thing for both of us at the time.

Through the years, I've played the conversation over and over in my mind from the night the decision was made. It was a Friday night and I'd gone up to spend the weekend with Linden. We were sitting in his bedroom in the apartment he shared with two other guys he went to school with. Linden was so loving, all the way up to the point that I became pregnant. I never saw it coming.

"I wonder if it's a girl or a boy," I said. He sat between my legs on the floor at the foot of the bed while I sat on the edge of the bed massaging his shoulders.

"Bree, I've been thinking."

"Thinking about what?"

"Well, I've been thinking about how fast everything is happening."

"Fast? We've been dating for a couple years, Linden."

"I know, but I've only got one more year before I'm finished school, Bree." Linden had turned around and was on his knees on the floor facing me. "And I think I will be more prepared for a child when I'm done."

I was stunned. "Linden, what would you like me to do? This wasn't a choice that I made. We both know that..."

"I know. I know. But we'll both be finished with school soon and we can get married and have a baby after that. Lets be smart, Bree. I don't want to end up like all the other couples who could have made something of their lives, but chose to have a baby instead."

"So what are we supposed to do about this baby?" I shuttered at the thought of what he was leading up to.

"Well, it's still early. We can have an abortion. I'll pay for it and I'll go with you, Bree."

"We? I asked.

"Yes. I will be right there with you every step of the way. I promise."

"What about you and me, Linden? I thought we had something special. I thought you loved me."

"Bree, you know I love you and that has nothing to do with the decision we have to make about our futures."

"Doesn't it, Linden?" I refused to cry. I never wanted it to be said that I used tears to coerce him into making a decision that he'd regret for the rest of his life.

I couldn't believe that Linden, who had claimed to love me so much, could possibly ask me to end the life that I had growing inside me. The life that he and I both created. But it was true. Linden didn't want anything to interfere with his law career and I didn't want to bring a child into this world under those circumstances, so I agreed to terminate the pregnancy. Linden paid for it and went with me as he agreed, but I never looked at Linden or life quite the same, and eventually, the warm feeling of love I had for him just turned sour. I couldn't look at Linden without thinking of the child we would've had together, and how his career took priority over us.

God, please take it all away. I don't want to be in this place in my life. Not again.

I closed my eyes tightly as the tears ran onto the pillow. The last thing I needed is more disappointment in my life. What if I decided to have this child and things didn't work out between Charles and me? What if I decided to tell him and he freaked out and told me this wasn't the right time in our lives to bring a child into the world? What if the Charles I thought I knew wasn't who I thought he was after all? What if *I* am not a good mother? Questions kept forming in my mind, but I didn't have any answers.

I felt a headache coming on and knew that I had to change my thoughts to something else. I thought about Granny and took in a deep breath. I yearned to smell her once again. She always smelled of soft perfume and vanilla scented candles. She'd developed a liking to them after we'd given her an assortment for a Mother's Day gift one year. Remembering her took my mind off the stressful things that were happening in my life at that moment and I finally began to relax enough to drift off into a deep sleep.

EIGHT

I awakened to the sound of voices coming from down the hall. Mama and Bliss were in a heated discussion about Bliss coming home at night. I turned over to find my sister Monica lying on her bed reading a magazine.

"Hey, sleepy head! I wondered how long you'd be asleep," she said sarcastically.

"Hey, girl! When did you get home? I thought you had to work today."

"I did. I got off at three. Got here about three-thirty. What time did you get home?" she asked, still flipping the pages of the *Essence*.

"Around noon. I went over to see Papa and Dee, then came home to take a nap. Whew! That trip is getting longer every time I come home!" I said, stretching from my nap.

"Mmm hmmm. Girl, that's only a three and a half hour drive. You must be getting old, because that's not enough time to make anyone sleepy."

Monica laughed and I threw the pillow at her.

"Whatever! So, where's your shadow?" I asked, referring to her twin, Veronica.

"At work. She won't be home until about five-thirty. She's been talking about seeing you. She'll be glad to come home and find *you* here."

"I can't believe I've been asleep for three hours. I only meant to take a short nap. What's going on with Mama and Bliss?" I asked.

"Nothing new. Those two are always at it. Ever since Bliss became a senior in high school, she's been thinking she's grown enough to stay out 'till damn near morning, and every now and then she thinks she can tip in here the next day and get away with it. I just laugh at 'em," Monica smirked.

Monica and Bliss never did get along. There were five years between Bliss and the twins, but you'd think they were closer in age when you considered the rivalry between them. Monica was jealous of the attention that Bliss got by being the baby of the family, while Bliss did all she could to piss her off just for the sake of it. In fact, I was surprised how different Monica and Veronica were from each other. While Dee and I stuck close together, they didn't seem to have that same bond that normally existed between twins. Veronica usually went off by herself, leaving Monica behind to pick on Bliss.

Actually, Chauntel and Bonita, who were twenty-five and twenty-six, acted more like twins than Monica and Veronica did. They were inseparable. The other twins, Joey and Joy, who were born two years after Dee and I, didn't share much of anything after they passed the toddler stage. Maybe that was because they were different sexes. We had our differences just like every other family, but overall we were close. I wasn't about to stand by and watch my baby sister ruin her life without at least trying to do something about it.

"Well, I don't see anything funny about it and Bliss won't either if she gets caught out there in something she can't get herself out of," I replied angrily.

"Maybe *you* can talk some sense into her while you're home because Mama's at her wit's end with that girl," Monica pleaded.

"I'll see what I can do," I said. "I promised to talk to Bliss before I headed back to Georgia."

I forced myself out of bed and walked across the room. I wanted to say hello to Bliss and see how she was doing. As I neared the end of the hall, I could see that she had closed her bedroom door after she and Mama exchanged words.

"Bliss, you in there?" I asked, tapping lightly on the door.

"It depends on who wants to know," Bliss replied, yanking the door open with a big smile on her face. "Hey, big sister! I saw your car in the driveway, but Mama immediately started getting on my case as soon as I walked in the house and I forgot just that quickly," Bliss snarled as she hugged my neck.

"So, how long are you gonna be home?" she inquired.

"I'll be here till Sunday. Charles is coming Friday and we're driving back together. So, what have *you* been up to lately, Miss High School Graduate?" I asked, trying to remain neutral about her and Mama.

"Well, as you know I'm all grown up now. I'm finished with school and onto bigger and better things. I'm trying to make some money so I can get my own place. You feel me?" Bliss replied as she stared into her mirror, playing with her shoulder length curly locks. She'd started wearing her hair in large, loose curls and always kept her nails manicured. In a lot of ways she reminded me of Camilla, except Bliss didn't have that bossy nature that Camilla had. She kept up with the leading fashions and always made sure she was picture perfect when she walked out the front door. I suppose the entertainment business called for that sort of thing.

"So what exactly are you doing to make money? Where are you working?" I asked, anticipating the answer.

"Working? Oh, well, I'm an entertainer. You remember how I always loved to dance and wanted to be in videos? Well, I finally got my big break and I'm dancing at a couple spots during the week. Now, it's just a start, but I'm making a *lot* of money and I'm going to be moving up to bigger and better things soon. You'll see."

"And what about college? Aren't you afraid of worrying your poor mother to an early grave? Why don't you…"

"See, I knew Mama would tell you. She doesn't even know any of the details," she shrieked.

I grabbed Bliss' arm to get her to calm down.

"Bliss, listen. That's just it; she *doesn't* know any of the details and that's what's bothering her. You're her baby girl and she doesn't want to see you get hurt," I said, trying to reason with her.

"But she doesn't even want to hear about it. She just gets all mad and starts talking about how I should want something better for my future and blah, blah, blah." Bliss rolled her eyes as though she had heard enough.

"Okay, then let me check it out and if everything's cool, I'll convince her that know you know what you're doing. How's that?" I suggested.

Bliss always thought of me as a cool older sister, and I did whatever I could to maintain a close relationship with her. I knew what it felt like to grow up without a father and how desperate a young woman could be for the security of a father figure and not have one to turn to. I hoped that my constant presence in her life would make a difference.

"Well, I dance at a place called The Leisure Lounge on Thursdays. It's over on Southside, and if you want to see what it's like you can stop by. I go on at eleven," she said nonchalantly and began filing her nails.

"There's one more thing. You never answered my question about college. Do you think you might wanna go?" I remained hopeful that she'd at least thought about it.

"Never really gave it much thought to tell you the truth. I met my manager, Pete, in my senior year and he told me I could make more money dancing, so I decided to give it a try and boom, I'm a star. Besides, I don't want to worry Mama with trying to pay for one more college education."

"Bliss, Mama didn't have to come out of her pocket for our college tuitions. She did take responsibility for *some* things, but those of us who decided to go to college worked and took out loans to pay for our *own* college tuition. And Dante was smart enough to get a scholarship, so he didn't have to worry about paying for *his* tuition."

"Well, I'm going to be a dancer, so what do I need to go to college for?" Bliss said as though *I* didn't understand.

It hurt to realize that my baby sister hadn't a clue what she was doing. All she saw were dollar signs and the material things she could have while getting paid for doing something she loved to do. She'd always been among the best dancers and cheerleaders in her group, but she was barking up the wrong tree now, and her ignorance about the things that go on in the business she's gotten into could land her in far more trouble than she realized.

"Well, I'll stop by tomorrow night to see the *star* perform, okay? Meanwhile, I'm gonna go downstairs and see what Mama needs help with. See you in a little bit."

I closed Bliss' door behind me and headed downstairs to check on Mama. I could smell a hint of cinnamon and the aroma of simmering, smoked meat coming from the kitchen. It smelled like Thanksgiving, but since it was the middle of June, I was a bit surprised. Mama stood over the stove stirring something in a big pot and suddenly it became apparent what I'd smelled on the way down. Mama was cooking her famous collard greens with smoked turkey.

"Mmm. What's with the collards, Mama? And I smell cinnamon. I know you're not baking pies." I went straight for the oven door and opened it slightly to peek in. Two golden sweet potato pies lay waiting to be devoured.

"They just need another ten minutes and then I'll take 'em out," she said proudly. "So did you get enough rest, sleepy head?" she continued.

"Yeah. I stayed up late last night and got up early, so I was exhausted," I lied, but with no intention of telling Mama about the pregnancy, I was pretty much out of choices.

"So, what've you been up to, Mama?" I asked, hoping she'd gotten some form of a social life started since I last saw her.

"Oh, just the usual. Keeping up the house, choir practice, and selling my pies and cakes. I've got a few dress orders that I'm working on right now, too, so I've been busy," she replied, piddling around with some dishes in the sink.

"That's nice. Maybe you'll become the next Mrs. Smith!" I said, jokingly. Mama laughed. "I know you had a hard time after Daddy died, trying to keep up with the mortgage and pay the other bills and keep food in the house. I just wanted to let you know that I really appreciate everything you did for us, Mama."

"Well, your Daddy's pension from UPS and his social security was a lifesaver. But, your brothers worked and helped out a whole lot, too. And we can't forget Granny and Papa; they helped out whenever things got tight. The money I made from baking and sewing just helped us with the *extra* things we needed."

"You did a great job holding our family together, Mama."

"Thanks, baby. I just wish I could've afforded to send all my babies to college."

"That's okay, Mama. It didn't stop us from going," I said as I rubbed her shoulder. "But what about *you*, Mama? Are you getting out at all with any of your friends?" I asked.

"Bree, I don't have time for stuff like that. I have to…"

"Any new men join the church lately?" I asked, cutting her off.

Mama stopped and looked at me. She knew where the conversation was going. I'd watched my mother suffer from depression for many years with the hope that someday she'd have a life outside of this house. Cooking, talk shows, and church were all she had going on and I'd hoped for many years that she'd meet someone who could make her feel special again. After all, she was only fifty-one years old and still a very attractive woman. She'd be a prime catch for any man.

"No new men at church, and I'm not even gonna ask why," she replied sternly.

"Mama, I just want you to be happy," I said, reaching out for her hand as she brushed past me to throw some scraps from the greens in the trash.

"I *am* happy, Bree. I'm right where I'm supposed to be. Don't you worry yourself about me," she remarked as she headed back to the sink to rinse her hands. "So, what are *you* going to do about calling Linden?" she asked, changing the subject.

"Let's go watch some television," I replied sarcastically.

I knew when Mama changed the subject I had to let it go because she wasn't going to allow me to continue drilling her with questions. We retired to the family room with glasses of iced tea and surfed through the channel guide until we found some back to back episodes of *Law and Order*, which we were happy to watch. For the next couple hours, we relaxed on the fluffy, oversized sofa until I decided to get ready to head out to Papa's for dinner and to help him sort through some of Granny's papers. I also looked forward to spending the night with Dee.

NINE

On the way over to Papa's house, I decided I'd return Linden's call to see what he wanted. Even though our relationship ended on a sour note, over the years we managed to move past the pain and at least remain civil to each other. We lived in the same city, but rarely saw each other and hadn't spoken in a while. Occasionally, he'd call during the holidays to check on everyone and to wish me well in the New Year, but that was the extent of our communication. When Linden and I went our separate ways, there was no going back. Not for me at least. I no longer had faith in him and for me that was very important. I needed to know that the man I loved had my back and would be there for me through thick and thin. After all, love isn't selfish. It's all about sacrificing and compromising, and Linden proved that those weren't the terms of our relationship. Yet, in spite of all that, there remained a special place in my heart for him. I tucked it away where even I would barely know it existed.

Reaching into my purse, I pulled out the sticky note with Linden's number on it and took a deep breath before dialing the number.

"Linden McAllister speaking."

I paused.

"Linden McAllister speaking," he said in a louder voice.

"Hi Linden. This is Breanna," I said hesitantly.

"Breanna. It's good to hear from you." Linden's voice softened.

"So you heard about Granny."

"Yes, and I want you to know how sorry I am and if there's anything at all I can do, please let me know."

"Thanks, Linden. That means a lot to me and my family."

"So, when's the funeral?" he asked.

"The service is Saturday at noon."

There was silence as if the call had dropped.

"So how are things going with you, Linden?" I asked, just as he inquired if I were free for lunch tomorrow.

We both laughed.

"You go first," Linden said.

"I just wanted to know how things were going with you. How's the job?" I said again.

"Well, that brings me to what I wanted to ask *you.* How about lunch tomorrow and we can talk about it then?"

I thought for a moment.

"Well, I promised Papa I'd help him out and I may have to run some errands for him tomorrow, so lunch probably won't be good for me," I replied

"Oh, okay," Linden said, sounding disappointed.

"But, if you're free later on tomorrow night, we can have dinner. How's that?" I asked.

"I think I can leave some time open for an old friend," he replied.

"So how does seven o'clock sound?"

"How about eight?" I asked, determined not to let him take control.

"Eight's fine. Should I pick you up?" he asked.

"No, I might be out, so I'll meet you," I replied.

Linden and I decided to meet at an old favorite wing spot on my side of town and said goodbye. Since I wasn't able to reach Camilla earlier I decided I'd call her back before I arrived at Papa's, so I dialed her cell phone, hoping she'd answer.

"Hey, Bree!" she answered, sounding excited.

"What's up, Mill?"

"I'm just eating a little dinner and trying to find something worth watching on television tonight. How was the drive?" she asked.

"It was okay. By lunchtime I'd gotten unbelievably sleepy. I took a nap and felt like I could've slept the day away," I said, yawning.

"I heard it does that to you. How's everybody doing?" she asked with concern.

"Everyone's okay. I'm headed to Papa's right now to help him go through some of Granny's papers. I'm going to spend the night with him and Dee tonight," I said.

"Oh, that should be nice. I'm sure Papa appreciates you being there."

"Mill, you're never going to believe who I just got off the phone with."

I paused.

"Who, Bree?" she asked.

"Linden," I answered.

"No you didn't! Whatever would you have to talk about with him at a time like this?" she asked with sarcasm.

"Okay, just calm down! He talked to Mama this morning after he heard about Granny and left his number for me to call. I just returned his call, that's all," I responded.

"Whew! That's a relief. I know you don't want to go down that road again," she said.

At that point, I decided I'd keep my dinner plans with Linden to myself. If not, I'd have Camilla whining in my ear all night with one hundred reasons why I shouldn't meet him. I had my own agenda though, and meeting Linden for dinner would be killing two birds with one stone.

"Well, Mill, I'm getting closer to the house, so I'm gonna go now."

I'd talked long enough and wanted to hang up the phone.

"Okay, Bree. I'll be there Friday night, okay?" she noted, as if I'd forgotten.

"Okay. I'll see you then," I replied.

"Smooches, babe," Camilla said before disconnecting call.

I chuckled and stuffed my cell phone in my purse. Camilla was quite a character. She always had my back and after the breakup between Linden and me, she didn't have a problem telling me she never liked him and relished the thought of him being out of the picture. I'd dated a few guys here and there and had a couple of boyfriends since then, but nothing serious until I'd moved to Georgia and met Charles. For some reason, she loved the idea of me being with Charles. She said it just felt "*right*" to her and that she felt in her spirit that Charles was the perfect man for me. Funny

TEN

I arrived at Papa's house just in time to see Aunt Geri backing out of the driveway. After pulling my car in, I ran over to the curb to give her a hug.

Hi, Bree! Look at you. Looks like Georgia's treating you quite well,"
she remarked.

"Thanks, Auntie. I hate that I missed you. I hoped we would have a chance to catch up."

"Papa told me you're staying tonight, so I'll come over in the morning for a cup of coffee, okay? Right now I have to get over here to Sonetta and Bill. I've been running around and I'm late starting dinner."

"Alright. See you in the morning." I waved as Aunt Geri drove to her house down the street.

Papa had gotten hungry and started fixing our plates the moment I walked in. He explained that Dee had already eaten dinner and that he waited until I got back. Over dinner, he talked non-stop about Granny and how she was so active down at the church, and how the members were saying they're going to miss her and her cooking. Then, he went on to tell me about the vegetable garden out back that she started and how he planned to keep it up throughout the rest of the summer.

I told Papa I thought he should take a break and relax and let someone else do some things around the house, but he was adamant about going on with life as usual.

"Your Granny would want it that way," he said.

After dinner, we moved to the living room where Papa had stacked the boxes we had to rummage through. We dug right in and before long, Papa and I were laughing and reminiscing about times we'd shared as a family. We came across old pictures that I'd forgotten were ever taken.

"Oh, my goodness! Look at this one of me and Dee with ponytails. We must've been about eight years old," I said as I handed the photo to Papa.

"Y'all were so cute. That picture was taken in the yard right out back. I can see one of my old push mowers in the distance," Papa said as he smiled and started telling his famous story about the collection of lawn mowers that he'd acquired over years.

While Papa proceeded to describe each and every lawn mower he'd ever owned, I continued to browse through old photos and letters. At the bottom of the box I came across a plain white envelope labeled "Sonetta" with photos of Granny holding a beautiful baby. She sat next to an attractive woman I'd never seen before and it looked as though the photos were taken in a hospital room. The fact that Sonetta was adopted has never been a secret, but I never knew that Granny knew her birth mother. Was the woman in the pictures Sonetta's birth mother? If so, why would she have given her away? I wondered if Papa knew the answers, but he was still engrossed in his lawn mower collection story and I didn't want to interrupt him, so I stuffed the pictures back into the envelope and tossed it into a nearby box marked "Scrapbook."

I suggested we put all the pictures in this box so that Mama could put them together in a scrapbook for Papa to keep. Old letters and cards and other important papers were placed in a box marked *Keepsakes*, and other things like receipts were placed in a trash bag. By the time we were done, hours had passed and I could hear sleep calling my name again.

"Papa, what's in that big yellow envelope?" I asked, pointing to a large envelope sitting on the sofa near him.

"This is one of the things I was looking for. Your grandmother recently sold some land that had been in her family for many years, and these are the documents the attorney needed to make the transaction final." Papa smiled.

"So the sale wasn't final?" I asked.

"The sale has been finalized for quite some time, but the attorney needs to distribute the funds from the account to the people she left it to. That's why he needs these documents. This is the errand I mentioned I needed you to take care of for me tomorrow. We have to take care of this as soon as possible." Papa handed me the clasped envelope, addressed to an attorney in Rock Hill.

"No problem. Rock Hill's only five minutes away. I'll take it in the morning," I said, tucking the envelope under my arm.

"Good night," I said as I kissed Papa good night before heading down the dark hallway leading to Dee's room at the back of the house.

ELEVEN

I tapped lightly on Dee's door before entering and find her sitting in her rocking chair watching Anderson Cooper on CNN.

"I'm back, Dee. Ready for me to do your hair?"

She continued rocking with her eyes glued to the television while I searched the room for her hair brush. I found one in her night stand and loosened her pony tail to begin sectioning her hair. I noticed that Dee had a few more strands of gray hair than I had, and wondered if that meant she had more stress than me. Sometimes I felt as though I were the one that suffered the most after Daddy's accident, and that Dee took the easy way out by closing herself off to the world. Watching her become this other person had never been easy and I often asked myself if she'd done it by choice.

"So, Dee – what's happening on Anderson Cooper tonight? Anything interesting?" I asked as I brushed one section of her hair.

No reply.

"Charles is coming Friday," I said, changing the subject.

Dee didn't seem to be the least bit interested in Charles coming. She continued watching television in silence, so I stopped talking and slid over to start on the other side of her naturally curly hair. Not much has changed about Dee's physical appearance and in spite of the years that have gone by, her flawless skin still has its glow; the same glow that drew people to her as a child and made her one of the most popular girls in high school.

In school everyone loved her, and the fact that she was outgoing *and* an "A" student made her even more fascinating. She charmed the teachers with her intellect and girls wanted to be her friend because she had everything going for her. She was intelligent and witty, and her beauty just added to her popularity. Guys at school found Deanna challenging and exciting, and her nonchalant attitude about them made them chase after her even more. She could take them or leave them, nor was she intrigued by them, but her attitude changed when we were fifteen years old.

Dee had become somewhat withdrawn and started spending lots of time to herself. She always had an excuse to go off on her own and rarely wanted to do the things we once enjoyed doing together or with our other brothers and sisters, like going bowling or to the movies. When I asked her about it, she'd brush it off as though she was too busy with homework or studying, but strangely enough her grades were also dropping. And she'd started avoiding me. Sometimes when I walked into our bedroom, she'd find a reason to leave. At times, I wondered if I'd done something to cause the detachment that we were going through, but I eventually blamed it on the fact that we were growing up and maybe even apart. Dee eventually confided in me that she had a boyfriend – someone older than her who went to a different school. She said he was the brother of one of her friends at school that I didn't know, and that they'd met over the telephone, but started going out when she visited her friend and met him in person. That's all the information she would give me about her secret love, and although I had no proof, I know that it must have ended badly because my Deanna became a totally different person. Everything inside of me knew that her perfect heart had been crushed.

She'd been through so much – a broken heart, then seeing Daddy die before her very eyes. My compassion for her pain was so strong that I almost wished I could join her in it so that she wouldn't be alone. Instead, I just stood there caressing her face and running my fingers through her hair, hoping that she understood just how much I loved her, until her head rested against the back of the rocking chair and she fell asleep.

I'd almost forgotten that I needed to call Charles before going to bed, so I tipped quietly off to the other side of the room with my purse and took a seat on the bed and dialed Charles' mobile number.

"Hi, baby! Did I wake you?" I asked

"I just dozed off a minute ago. How's everything going there?" He yawned.

"Okay so far. I'm at Papa's. We went through some of Granny's things tonight and I have to run an errand for him tomorrow. That's about it. What's going on there?" I asked.

"Well, let me see. Work was the same as usual. Oh, you got a package in the mail today; looks like it might be a book. And did I tell you I miss you so much that I'm sleeping in your tee shirt tonight?"

"Yeah, right!" I smirked. "You can't even fit into my tee shirts," I said.

"Okay, so I lied about the tee shirt, but I'm not lying about missing you, baby. I can't wait for Friday so I can head to Charlotte." His voice turned serious.

"I miss you, too, Charles, and I'll call you tomorrow to see how you're doing. But right now, I can barely keep my eyes open, so I'm gonna call it a night," I said, yawning into the receiver.

"Not if I call you first. Love you, baby," he added.

"Love you, too," I replied.

Charles blew me a kiss and we hung up.

I do love Charles. Being away from him made me realize just how much I cared about him and how much I've come to rely on him being an everyday part of my life. Still, something inside told me to proceed with caution. I was still expecting someone to pull the rug out from under my feet any moment and tell me that it was all a dream. That would make more sense to me than this did.

I lay back on Dee's bed in a fetal position and listened as the voices from the television grew faint and I fell off to sleep.

TWELVE

I was awakened by bright rays of sun shining through the bedroom window directly into my face. Squinting from the light, I reached over to the night stand and fumbled around for the alarm clock. I just knew that I'd overslept, but it was only seven thirty and I had plenty of time to get started with my plans for the day.

I needed to freshen up, so I scrambled to the bathroom for a quick shower before doing anything else. I treated myself to one of my favorite tropical shower creams and slipped into some light cotton pants and a tee to help me survive the Carolina heat. The temperature was usually higher in Fort Mill and I'd seen the forecast indicating a high of ninety degrees for today. There was nothing worse than being overdressed in extreme temperatures.

As I stuffed my dirty clothes and toiletry bag back into my overnight bag, the aroma of freshly brewed coffee crept into the bedroom, and I craved a cup. I headed to the kitchen to find Aunt Geri sitting at the table anxiously awaiting the coffee Papa was pouring into her mug.

"Good morning, Bree." Aunt Geri beamed.

"Good morning. Where's Dee?" I asked, walking over to the window.

"On the sun porch. That's her favorite morning spot."

"Got a cup ready for me?" I asked, turning to Papa.

"Right here." Aunt Geri pointed to a mug on the table across from her.

"Care for some breakfast, Bree?" she asked.

"No, thanks. I'm gonna have one of these bananas," I said, reaching into the fruit bowl on the counter. I wanted to avoid anything that could cause morning sickness and fruit seemed like the best way to do it.

"So what time do your day care clients start arriving, Auntie?" I inquired.

"The earliest one comes around eight, but she had an appointment this morning, so she'll be a little late. I've got a few minutes before I have to get back. So what's new with you and that good-looking boyfriend of yours? Y'all got any wedding plans yet?" she asked, smiling as she sipped coffee from her mug.

"Not yet, Auntie," I replied, almost choking as I was caught off guard. "Right now, I'm involved in a special project at work and it's taking up a lot of my time. Maybe someday," I answered.

"Well, don't take too long, Bree. Aren't you about thirty now?" she asked.

"Yes, but I still have plenty of time," I replied

"Leave the girl alone, Geraldine," Papa interjected.

"I'm just saying…" she began before Papa cut her off.

"She's got plenty of time to think about stuff like that. Not everyone desires to be married and have children, you know," he added

"That's right, Auntie. *Some* women are okay with being single and concentrating on their careers," I continued.

"If you say so," Aunt Geri concluded, while sipping coffee from her mug.

"So, what's on your plate today, Bree?" Papa asked, changing the subject.

"I have that errand to run this morning, and then I'm going to head home and see what everyone else is getting into today. Oh, and I'm having dinner with an old friend this evening. This reminds me, I'd better get going."

Whew! Saved by the bell. Thanks Papa!

I poured the rest of the coffee into the sink and placed the mug in the dishwasher. After getting my bags from Dee's room, I went into the living room and picked up the scrapbook box. After kissing Papa and Aunt Geri, I went out on the sun porch to tell Dee I was leaving and headed out.

"Papa, I might stop by later this afternoon. See you later Aunt Geri," I yelled as I headed out the side door.

I put the scrapbook box and my overnight bag in the trunk and I glanced at my watch to check the time.

Nine o' clock.

I found the traffic to be surprisingly light as I merged onto the interstate headed south. My drive to Rock Hill took less than ten minutes and before I knew it, I was pulling into the parking lot at the professional building where the attorney's office was located. As I entered the office, a young and very attractive receptionist glanced up from her computer monitor and smiled.

"May I help you?" she asked as stood to greet me.

"Yes, I'm here to see Attorney Simmons."

"Is he expecting you?" she inquired.

"Not exactly, I don't think. I'm here to drop off this package for my grandfather. His name is Barnett Baker," I said, holding up the envelope.

"Oh. Mr. Baker! Have a seat. Attorney Simmons will be right with you," she said, smiling as if she knew my uncle personally.

She left the reception area for a moment and returned with a short, stout man.

"Are you Mr. Baker's granddaughter?" he asked, extending his hand toward mine.

"Yes," I answered as I was met with his firm grip.

"I'm Attorney Hugh Simmons. Come right this way," he directed.

I followed him into a large, but cluttered office, where several stacks of law books and file folders took up most of the walking space. Attorney Simmons closed the door behind me and took a seat at his desk.

"I was sorry to hear about the loss of your grandmother. Please accept my condolences."

"Thank you, Mr. Simmons."

"She was a fine woman. I've known your grandparents for many years and I know she will be missed," he added.

"My grandfather wanted me to bring you this envelope," I said as I placed it on his desk.

Attorney Simmons opened the envelope and began to examine the documents inside.

"I helped your grandmother finalize the sale of her land and we never got around to transferring the funds. She signed all the necessary paperwork though. Now all we have to do is distribute the proceeds equally amongst you all," he murmured.

"You mean my grandmother left us some money?" I asked, surprised.

"She sure has. A nice little bit I might add. Your grandparents had gotten some good advice about some land she inherited from her family and she held out until the developers offered her top dollar for it," he added as he studied the last of the documents in the envelope.

"Well, looks like everything is all here. I'll get these over to the bank today and I should have the checks for you tomorrow around this same time," he said as he stuffed the documents back into the envelope.

I stood and thanked him for his time and told him I'd return in the morning. The receptionist smiled as I passed her desk.

"Tell your grandfather I said hello," she said as I opened the door.

"I will. Thanks."

I thought about the conversation with Attorney Simmons all the way to Mama's house.

Well, I'll be damned! Who would've guessed that Granny would leave us some money?

Finally, something positive happened this week. And If I can get through the rest of this week and still have my sanity, that would be a major accomplishment.

THIRTEEN

I was pleasantly surprised to find my sisters, Chauntel and Bonita, at Mama's house when I arrived. The two had taken the rest of the week off from work to help with funeral arrangements and to run whatever errands they could for Papa. We hugged and gathered in the kitchen while Mama made a grocery list of items needed from the store to take over to Papa's house. Everyone in the town of Fort Mill knew Granny, and Papa was sure to become inundated with people dropping by soon to give their condolences, leave food, or offer to help in any way they can.

"So how's life in Greensboro, Bonita?" I asked.

"Everything is good. You should make good on your promise to come visit me. You still haven't seen my apartment," Bonita snickered.

"I know and I'm sorry. We've been really busy with a huge project at work and it has taken just about all of my time for the past six months. Hopefully things will get wrapped up in the next couple of months and I can get back to life as usual," I assured her.

"Good, because I was beginning to take it personal."

We both laughed.

"What about you, Chauntel? And how are my babies doing?" I asked, interrupting as she and Mama mapped out the trip to Wal-Mart in advance.

"Growing like weeds. They'll be turning two soon and you know what that means," Chauntel said as she added paper cups to the grocery list Mama had made.

"Oh no. The dreaded terrible twos. I hope you and Brian have locked all the cabinets and drawers," I said.

"Girl, you don't know the half of it. The other day Kendra got her hands on one of my lipsticks and had Kendrick's face covered in it. You should've seen 'em laughing."

"Now, *that* was a Kodak moment," Mama said, laughing until her sides hurt.

"Don't think I didn't get my cell phone just in time to snap a picture." Chauntel said as she removed the phone from the holster and scrolled through it hysterically.

We all took our turns looking at the pictures and laughing at the twins.

"I can't wait to see 'em," I said.

"Well, you'll get your wish Saturday. Hopefully, they won't tear the place down," she replied.

"So, Bree, how'd everything go at Papa's last night?" Mama asked.

"Good. I just helped him sort through some of Granny's papers. Oh, and I did Dee's hair." I shrugged as though it were no big deal.

I decided not to mention the envelope or my visit to Attorney Simmons. I figured Papa would want to do the honors of surprising everyone with their gifts from Granny, especially since he never specified who the money from the sale was for.

After checking to make sure she had everything on the list, Mama suggested we head out to Wal-Mart before it started getting crowded. We grabbed our purses and headed for the front door.

"Who's driving?" Mama asked.

"Well, since I'm near the end of the driveway, we can take my car," I replied, searching for my keys.

We spent only the time that was needed in Wal-Mart to pick up the items on the grocery list. Mama wanted to take everything straight to Papa's so that we could sit down and discuss the program for the funeral, so we headed to Fort Mill.

Papa was surprised to see us pulling into the driveway. He appeared to have been pulling up weeds from the flower beds underneath the windows.

"What are you ladies doing here?" he asked, smiling and removing his gardening gloves as he walked toward us.

"Chauntel and Bonita! Good to see you," he said as he kissed each of them.

"Hi, Papa. We picked up some things from Wal-Mart to help out. It might get a little busy around here," Bonita replied.

Mama and I removed the bags from the trunk and everyone grabbed a couple to take into the house.

"Papa, I'm going to sit the paper cups and plates here on the counter next to the napkins and plastic forks," I said, arranging everything neatly.

"And where do you want us to put the cases of sodas?" Mama asked.

"Let's stack 'em inside the refrigerator so they'll get nice and cold," he suggested.

Chauntel and Bonita were already on their way to the back of the house to see Dee. When Mama and I finished setting everything up, she asked Papa if he felt up to talking about the program. He agreed that we needed to get it outlined and off to be printed as soon as possible, so he called Aunt Geri and asked her to come over to help put it together.

Papa sat the pound cake on the table that Mama brought over yesterday and we each enjoyed a slice while we discussed the service from beginning to end. It had already been decided that the program would be entitled, "The Home Going Service of Beulah Mae Baker" and that it would take place on Saturday at noon at Trinity Baptist Church in Fort Mill where Granny and Papa have been members for years. Aunt Geri suggested that the Senior Choir sing Granny's favorite song, *Peace Be Still*. She also said that she'd gotten a call from Granny's sister, Aunt Mary Jo, requesting to sing *Amazing Grace.* My four brothers and Granny's brothers, Uncle Jessie and Uncle Howard, would be Pallbearers, and the Pastor, Reverend Armstrong, would deliver the eulogy.

After completing the home going program, we chose the pictures we'd use, then put our heads together and wrote a beautiful obituary for Granny. I volunteered to take the program and obituary back to Mama's house and format it on my laptop.

"You brought your laptop?" Chauntel laughed.

"Actually, I don't leave home without it," I replied seriously.

"I'll take it to a copy service when I'm done to have it printed. How many copies do you think we'll need, Aunt Geri?" I asked.

"Better get about three hundred to be safe," she replied.

"And, Bree, don't forget to add that the interment will be at Evergreen Cemetery, and that the family repast will follow in the church's multi-purpose room," she added.

"Got it." I jotted the additional information on the paper and stuck it in my purse.

"Has anyone picked out Granny's clothing for the funeral home?" I asked, not wanting to leave anything out.

"Daddy and I are picking out something today and taking it over to Cunningham's Funeral Home tomorrow afternoon." Aunt Geri cried and Mama put her arms around her.

"Geri, we're all here for you and Papa. We know you're going to miss her. We all are. But we *will* get through this." Mama gave her a napkin to wipe her eyes.

"Thanks, Mayva," Aunt Geri said as she dabbed her eyes with the napkin.

"We'd better get going. We've got a lot to do." Chauntel hugged Aunt Geri and Papa.

Papa walked us to the car and quietly asked if I'd met with Attorney Simmons. I winked my eye and told him that I had everything under control.

"I don't know about y'all, but I'm famished," Mama said as we pulled out of the driveway.

"I am, too! Let's go have some lunch," Bonita suggested.

"Where to?" I asked.

"How about Panera Bread? I'm feeling like something fresh..." Chauntel said.

"Sounds good to me. What about you, Mama?" I asked, looking in the rearview mirror.

"Panera works for me. I just need to get *something* in my stomach," she responded.

I headed in the direction of the closest Panera Bread location. We ordered sandwiches and salads and enjoyed a few moments of laughter, which was just what we needed before heading back to Mama's house to format the program for Granny's home going service.

FOURTEEN

I spent the rest of the afternoon creating an extraordinary program for Granny's home going service. The photos of Granny that we selected at Papa's were scanned and placed on the program, one on the front cover and the others as a collage inside the program with the obituary at the center of everything. After adding a few finishing touches, I called everyone in to get their approval. We all agreed that the program was perfect, so I saved my work and began calling around for estimates on the printing cost. Determined not to skimp on anything to do with Granny's home going service, I decided on a smaller printing company who would use extra care printing the program. They even agreed to have one of their work order consultants hand deliver the finished programs at no additional cost. I thought to myself: *Now that's personalized service!*

I was almost sold on their service, but would make a final decision after checking out some of their sample work. They'd be open late enough for me to drop by on my way to meet Linden for dinner, so I emailed the file to the address they'd given me and decided on what time I'd start getting ready so I could squeeze that in on the way.

Glancing at the time, I realized that evening was drawing near and I wanted to get a nap in before meeting up with Linden. After shutting down the laptop, I turned over on the bed and faced the window. Time was passing by so quickly and soon it would be Saturday, and we'd be having Granny's funeral. I hoped my family would hold themselves. You always hear how some family member lost it at a funeral, either an uncle who came to the funeral drunk and embarrassed the entire family on the microphone, or an aunt who refused to let go of the casket and had to be dragged away by an usher or a family member. I truly hoped none of that would take place on Saturday, but you could never be sure, so I decided I'd be prepared for the worst. My eyelids became heavy as I listened to the sound of the humming from the lawn mower next door. The sound grew fainter as I drifted off to sleep.

Bam. Bam. Bam.

The sudden banging on the door caused me to jump up out of my sleep.

"What the heck…" I said, grabbing my chest as though I were having a heart attack.

"Monica! Telephone!" My sister Veronica shouted through the door.

"Take a message and tell them I'll call back," Monica mumbled as she turned over in her bed.

"What? What time is it?" I picked up my mobile phone to check the time.

Six thirty! I'm running a half-hour late!

I wanted to be out the door at least by seven so that I'd have a chance to stop at the printing company and check out the sample before meeting Linden. I jumped out of bed and went through my bags, grabbing my tropical scented shower gel and lotion, and the jeans and blouse I decided to wear. Luckily, they were hung in the garment bag and didn't need ironing.

I grabbed a towel and washcloth from the linen closet in the hall and hurried into the bathroom to jump in the shower. The combination of the warm jets of water and the scent of the tropical shower gel awakened my senses and brought me back to life.

Mmmm.

I wished I could spend an hour simply indulging in the luxury of a hot bath at that moment, but time didn't permit me to spend more than ten minutes in the tub or I'd risk being inconsiderately late. If there's one thing I had a pet peeve about, it was being late. I hate waiting for long periods of time, so I'd decided long ago that I'd be more considerate when it came to other people's time.

After my shower, I scrambled back to Monica's room to lotion down and get dressed. After applying a light foundation, eye shadow, and mascara, I touched up my hair, slid into my heels, and headed for the door. On the way out, I stopped in the family room to tell Mama that I was headed out to run some errands and meet a friend for dinner and would probably be back late. By the time I pulled out of the driveway it was seven fifteen, which was perfect timing to make a stop.

I only had to travel three exits north on the interstate to the printing company. I was greeted by a frail, older woman named Evelyn, who showed me some samples of programs they'd printed. I felt their quality of work was excellent and I placed an order for three hundred color programs for Granny's home going service.

"This is a beautiful creation," Evelyn said as she viewed the file I'd sent her.
"Who made this?" she asked.

"I did. Do you think I have a chance in this business?" I asked jokingly.

"You sure do! If you ever need a job, you come see me," she replied.

After giving her Mama's address where they could deliver the order tomorrow, I gave her my credit card information. Evelyn gave me a money back guarantee, but I knew I wouldn't be disappointed. After all, they'd been in the business over thirty years and from my conversation with her, I learned that they had some pretty decent companies as regular clients.

Glancing down at my watch, I noticed that it was almost seven fifty-five. At this rate, I should arrive at the wing spot to meet Linden at around ten minutes after eight, which was fashionably late, so there's no reason to rush at this point. Things were falling right into place just as I'd planned, but for some reason I'd started to feel nervous the moment I pulled out of the parking lot and onto the interstate headed south. Something inside told me that this would be a long night.

FIFTEEN

I pulled into the parking lot of the wing spot just in time to see Linden walking inside. I decided to park far enough away so that I could touch up my hair and makeup without being seen. There was no romance on my agenda for this meeting with Linden, but it *has* been a long while since we've seen each other and just like any other woman, I wanted to look my best when facing my ex-boyfriend so he'd have something to think about when we parted. It was just an innocent little "mind" game that women play - nothing out of the ordinary.

As I walked in the door, I could see Linden's eyes light up in the booth at the far right corner of the dining room. We both smiled as I walked toward him.

"Hi, Lin!" I said as he stood to greet me.

We hugged for a moment.

"Bree, you look more stunning than the last time I saw you!"

"Thank you!" I began to blush.

"You're looking pretty good yourself," I complimented in return.

"Well, I try to stay fit. Gotta stay in shape to fight off the criminals," he said.

"But, look at *you*! Hair flowing, skin glowing, and beautiful as ever," he remarked as he grabbed my hands.

There we go with that word "glowing" again. What the heck do they mean?

"No wedding band? You mean no one has swept you off your feet yet?" he asked.

"Not quite," I replied.

"What about you? Have you gotten yourself hitched yet?" I asked.

"Still a bachelor, for now." Linden squeezed my hands and asked if I wanted to order something to drink.

"I'm shocked that you even had to ask! You know I can't resist their famous pineapple lemonade!" I said as I looked around for the waitress.

"Guess I didn't know how much things had changed," Linden said as he summoned the waitress, who came over and asked if she could take our drink orders.

"We'll have two large pineapple lemonades," Linden said as he studied the waitress.

"I'll be right back with your drinks," she said, heading toward the fountain behind the counter.

"All jokes aside, Bree. I was so sorry to hear about your grandmother's passing. When I saw Kory uptown Monday evening and he told me the bad news, I thought of you immediately and called your mother first thing Tuesday morning to see how I could get in touch with you. I have to admit, I was glad to hear that you were on your way up from Atlanta, because I wanted to see you." Linden's smile had faded into a more serious look.

"Why? Is everything okay?" I asked.

"Yeah. Things are fine. I've just been thinking about you these last few weeks and I've wondered if you were okay," he replied.

"That's sweet of you, Linden. I've been fine. Working hard on a major project at work, but aside from that, everything was going fine until I got the news about Granny." I began to fumble with some napkins on the table.

"I'm sure the news was hard on everyone. How's your grandfather doing?" he asked.

"Well, you know Papa. He's going to try to hold it together for the family. He's being so strong, it's unbelievable," I said as I felt my eyes well up with tears.

"Bree, please let me know if there's anything I can do." Linden leaned over the table with a napkin just in time to wipe the tear that fell from my eye. Just then, the waitress returned, holding our drinks with a confused look on her face as if she wasn't quite sure what she'd just walked in on.

"Y'all ready to order?" she asked with her pen ready to go to work on her order pad.

"Shall I do the honors?" Linden asked, holding up the menu.

"Sure. Go right ahead," I said, humoring him.

"We'll have the combination tray with teriyaki, buffalo, and spicy garlic wings. I'll have an order of fried mushrooms with ranch sauce, and an order of loaded fries for the lady."

"Wow! I'm impressed. You remembered my favorites," I said enthusiastically.

“How could I forget? We were here almost every Friday night that I was in town,” he replied as he sipped his lemonade.

“Yep. You’re right,” I said, not knowing how else to respond to his comment.

“Linden, there *is* something you can do, if you’re willing to give me some of your time tonight,” I said matter-of-factly.

“Are you serious?” he asked.

“No, silly! I want to know if you’ll go somewhere with me. There’s something I need to check out and I’d rather not go alone, but I need someone I can trust,” I responded.

“Well, where?” he asked.

“Ever heard of the Leisure Lounge over on Southside?” I asked.

“Yeah, but why the hell would you want to go there? It’s not the classiest place in town. Now, I know a better place I can take you, where it’s more…” Linden started.

“Thanks, but I’m not going for enjoyment. There’s someone I’d like to see, but like I said, I’d rather not go alone. Are you going to go or not?” I asked.

“Sure. No problem,” he said as he picked up his lemonade and stared at me over his glass.

The waitress returned with the wing tray and our side orders and asked if we needed anything else.

“We’re good for now,” Linden replied.

We continued to catch up while we ate. Linden told me all about his adventures as a corporate attorney and I told him all about the project I was spearheading at my job. I was happy to hear of his success as an attorney. God knows that this was something he would have given up anything to have, and no matter how charming he appeared tonight, there would be no way that I'd forget that his career was at the very top of his list of priorities.

Before we knew it, almost two hours had passed since we'd met for dinner. It was nearly ten o' clock, but there was still an hour before Bliss' scheduled time to perform at the Leisure Lounge.

"So did you have a specific time you wanted to head over to the Leisure Lounge, or would you like to go for a drink somewhere?" Linden asked, reaching for his wallet to pay the bill.

"It's still a little early, but…"

"Oh – I know! We can stop at Dairy Queen for a Sunday on the way to Southside, if that's okay with you of course." Linden sounded like a kid with a new toy – excited to get it out of the package so that he could start playing with it.

"I guess by the time we get there I might have a taste for it," I replied.

"Why don't you leave your car here, Bree. After we leave the Leisure Lounge, I'll bring you back here to pick it up," he suggested.

I didn't see any harm in that, so I told him to lead the way. Linden's BMW was parked across the parking lot all by itself. He took extra precautions so that no one would ding his door getting into their car. I should've known he'd have something classy. After all, what's a lawyer without a Beamer?

The pit stop at Dairy Queen turned out to be nice after all. My hot fudge sundae was a cool treat in the heat of the night, not to mention the craving I had for something sweet.

By ten-thirty, I was ready to get over to the Leisure Lounge to see Bliss dance, so we finished up and headed toward Southside. I wasn't exactly sure what surprises lied ahead of me tonight, but I was ready to get it over with.

SIXTEEN

Linden turned into a parking lot that was adjacent to the club on the other side of the street. I noticed a few guys, maybe in their twenties, standing outside the club talking. The parking lot was full, so I expected that the club would be packed inside.

"You sure you want to go in?" Linden asked as he shut off the car engine.

"I don't really have a choice," I responded, reaching for my purse.

"I hope you're not going in here to catch some guy cheating! If so, let me know before I get inside," Linden said jokingly as he opened the passenger door for me.

"It's nothing like that. I need to see someone and I need you to promise me that whatever happens here tonight won't go any further." I gave him a serious look.

"I mean it! Promise me," I demanded.

"Okay, okay! I promise. But now you've got me even more confused," he replied.

One of the young guys standing outside opened the front door for me as I approached the building. Once inside, Linden and I came face to face with a bouncer who looked us over before passing us on to the next phase of entry, which was the desk where you paid your ten dollar cover charge. After Linden took care of the bill, we were free to enter.

The club itself wasn't a bad looking place. An L-shaped bar was situated near the entrance, and to the right of where we stood were a couple pool tables. Straight ahead past the bar, there was a runway which led to a stage that extended out into the audience, where round tables were set up randomly and counters with tall bar stools lined the walls. Music was blaring from the DJ booth on the opposite wall of where we stood by the entrance, and some people danced on the floor, while others drank and socialized at their tables or around the bar.

I looked at my watch and saw that it was ten forty-five, so I figured Bliss was somewhere getting ready to perform.

"You wanna get a drink?" Linden asked as he led me to two empty seats at the bar?

"I'll just have a ginger-ale," I replied.

"Ginger-ale? You sure that's it?" he asked as if I might be kidding.

"Yeah. I don't feel like drinking tonight," I lied. I knew enough to know that you're not supposed to drink when you're pregnant, but I had no intention of telling Linden about that.

"What can I get you?" the bartender asked as he placed two napkins in front of us.

"I'll have a double shot of Hennessy and a ginger-ale on ice for the lady," Linden replied.

"A double, huh? You sure you can handle that?" I asked.

"Well, I'm not exactly sure what's going to take place tonight and I need to relax a little. I'll sip it slow if it makes you feel any better." We both laughed and got comfortable in our seats.

The music was sounding good and I found myself tapping my hands on the bar and moving my feet to the beat.

"You wanna dance?" Linden asked.

"No, thanks. I'm just waiting for the show to start at eleven," I replied.

Just as I declined Linden's offer to dance, the lights were dimmed and the DJ began to speak on the microphone.

"All the brothers in the house give it up for our next performer. She hails from right here in the queen city of the south, Charlotte, North Carolina. Give it up for the one! The only! Venus!"

At that moment, the music started and Bliss came strutting down the runway like Beyonce, wearing a sheer robe tied at the waist with a silver, metallic roped belt and silver stilettos. When she reached the stage in the center of the room, she yanked the belt open, revealing a silver metallic two-piece bra and thong set connected by silver chains. She had on a long silky black wig that really made her look sexy and mysterious.

The crowd roared as she removed the sheer robe and threw it to the floor. I was in awe of my baby sister standing there exposed, looking like a woman. Her body was obviously that of a young, inexperienced girl. She was tight as a drum with a rock hard abdomen. No stretch marks from weight gain or pregnancy. No cellulite. She was perfect.

Bliss had captured everyone's attention in the building, including Linden, who was practically salivating at the vision of beauty on the stage before him.

"What do you think of her?" I asked, barely able to get Linden's attention.

"She's alright," he replied as he took a sip of Hennessy.

"Just alright?" I asked.

"Well, to be honest, she's fine as hell. But she's a little young for my taste," he admitted.

"Besides, I'd never be interested in a woman who worked in a place like this for a living," he added.

"Linden, that's my sister, Bliss, up there," I confessed.

"What the… teenage Bliss… baby-sister-who-wanted-to-follow-you-everywhere-you-went Bliss?" He was in total disbelief of what I was saying.

"She has always wanted to be a dancer and she's so naïve about this whole club dancing thing. She thinks this is going to lead to her becoming some big video queen." I briefed Linden on the fact that I told Mama I'd try to talk some sense into her before she ends up in a situation that she can't get out of.

"Well, she sure seems to be good at what she does," he remarked as his attention turned once again to Bliss.

She showed off all her sensual moves on stage. Men and young guys were watching as she dropped down to the floor and gyrated her hips to the beat, and when she turned around with her back toward the crowd and dropped down low on the stage, I saw one guy slap her butt cheeks and stick a bill in her thong. By this time, several guys had approached the stage and were all throwing bills at her. Some summoned her to come to them so they could stick a bill in her bra or thong and after she'd taken it, she'd move on to the next one.

The women in the crowd looked at her with complete envy and hatred. To them, she was just an object of erotic beauty that was definitely going to be competition for any woman who was there with her man tonight.

I'd seen all I wanted to see and I motioned to Linden that I was ready to leave.

"I'm sure you're enjoying the show, but I've seen just about enough," I said as I grabbed my purse and made my way toward the same door we'd come in through.

"You'll need a stamp on your hand if you're going to come back in," the bouncer said as we approached the door.

"No thanks. We're gone for the night," Linden replied as he opened the front door.

I was instantly relieved the moment we stepped outside. The air was clear from the smoke and smell of the sweaty men who got all worked up from watching the show.

"You okay, Bree?" Linden asked as he put his arm around my shoulder.

"I'm fine. I just had to see for myself and I'm so not okay with this," I replied as I shook my head in disbelief.

"How long has this been going on?" he asked.

"I'm not really sure, but I think it's been a few months. She mentioned her manager's name Tuesday when we talked. I think it was Pete. She said he approached her in her senior year and told her she'd make a lot of money dancing and that's how it all started."

"Somebody's got to get her away from this scene before something happens to her. You know what kind of people are in there and would take advantage of a young, naïve girl like her." Linden was beginning to scare me.

"I know. I don't even wanna think about what could happen. I'll talk to her again tomorrow. I told her I'd give it a chance and she invited me to come by and check out the show, but there's no way I'm going to co-sign for this mess."

My disgust turned to fear, which then turned to anger.

"Linden, can we please get out of here? I just wanna go."

We crossed the street and headed in the direction of Linden's car. As we pulled out of the parking lot, I took one last look at The Leisure Lounge and hoped I'd never have to see that place again.

SEVENTEEN

The ride back to the restaurant parking lot to get my car was considerably quiet. Linden knew me well enough to know not to bring up what he had seen at the club. He knew that seeing my baby sister standing on stage in the middle of a place like that, wearing almost nothing, with men clawing at her body and imagining doing all kinds of things to her sickened my stomach. I wanted to see Bliss succeed and I need to know that she's safe from harm, but I knew if this didn't stop, there would never be any peace about her. Not with me. Not with Mama. And if my brothers ever find out, there's going to be hell.

I wondered if there were anything I could've done to prevent this from happening. Maybe if I'd come home more often in the past year, she would've come to me before making the decision to go through with this. Maybe if I'd spent more quality time with her and been more of a role model to her, she would know that she doesn't have to sink to this level to fulfill her dreams.

"You okay?" Linden asked as he pulled into the parking space next to my car.

"Yeah. I just have a lot on my mind. This thing with Bliss tonight and then Granny's funeral on Saturday. It's a lot to digest, you know?" I replied.

"I know it has to be," he said, turning to face me in his seat.

"I feel like I'm responsible. I should've been here more…" Linden cut me off before I could finish my sentence.

"Now wait a minute, Bree. You can't go blaming yourself for the choices that other people make about their lives," he said.

"But…" I tried to speak.

"But nothing! Bree, for as long as I've known you, you have always taken on the responsibility of everything that ever happened to anyone you loved. I watched you do it with your mother's depression and with your sister Deanna."

I finally heard what he'd been thinking all these years.

"But Linden, they're my family!" I shouted.

"It doesn't matter, Bree, you cannot save everyone!" he shouted back.

"Besides, if you're busy saving everyone else, who's saving you?" Linden's voice went back down to a whisper and he placed his hands on my face.

"Let me help you," he said.

"Wha… what are you suggesting?" I asked with tears flowing down my face.

"Let me be here for you, Bree. Let me hold you and just be here for you. There's history between us and maybe we can try again," he said as he wrapped his arms around me.

Being in Linden's arms felt good after what I'd seen tonight, and as much as I needed consoling, I had to pull away from him before he tried to take things further.

"Thanks, Linden. You've really been a good friend tonight. Thanks for going with me even though you didn't have a clue what you were getting yourself into. Thanks for dinner and thanks for dessert. I appreciate everything," I said as I dried my eyes.

"But..." Linden waited for my reply.

"But, you said the key word – history. What we had was in the past and there's someone special in my life," I finished.

"You're not wearing a wedding band," he rebutted.

"No, but we currently live together. He's a wonderful man and I love him," I replied.

"Where is he tonight? Why isn't he here?" Linden asked.

"He's still in Georgia, but he'll be here tomorrow evening," I replied.

"Linden, let's not spoil things. There's history between us and we've had some good times in the past. You were very special to me, but I've moved on just as I'm sure you have." I explained.

"I'm being rejected, aren't I?" Linden cocked his head to the side and poked out his bottom lip like a child begging for candy.

"Thanks so much for everything, Linden," I said as I reached for my purse on the floor.

Linden grabbed my hand and gave it a squeeze.

"I'm glad we had a chance to catch up with each other. Unfortunately, it had to be under such grim circumstances, but it's good to see you again, nevertheless. You take care of yourself, Bree," he said.

"You do the same. Bye, Linden," I replied as I slid out of the passenger seat.

I didn't realize until I'd gotten out of the car that I felt as though I were suffocating while inside. I took a deep breath as I got into my own car and started the ignition. Linden and I waved goodbye and pulled out of the parking lot to go our separate ways.

What a draining night.

Suddenly, I wanted so badly to hear Charles' voice. Searching anxiously in my purse for my mobile phone, I finally found it hidden under my wallet and fumbled to dial Charles' mobile number. I let it ring five times and just as I was about to hang up in disappointment, I heard Charles' groggy voice on the other line.

"Hello," he said as though he weren't sure who was calling.

"I'm sorry I woke you, Charles. I know it's late; I just wanted to hear your voice." I apologized, but kept talking.

"What's going on, babe? Is everything okay?" Charles sounded worried.

Just then, tears began flowing uncontrollably down my cheeks.

"Everything is okay. I just miss you and I need to see you," I sobbed.

"Well, my flight is scheduled to arrive at ten minutes after seven tomorrow evening. But if you need me to, I can drive to Charlotte tonight. Just say the word," he offered.

"No, no. That's not necessary. It's late and you're already asleep. I'll pick you up from the airport tomorrow evening like we planned."

"So what are you doing out so late? Night out on the town?" he asked.

"I met up with one of my old friends from college and we hung out for a little while, but I'm exhausted so I'm heading back to the house." I cringed as the words came out of my mouth.

It wasn't exactly a lie. Linden and I *did* date in college, but I wasn't about to tell Charles that I just had dinner, dessert, and a trip down memory lane via the strip club with my ex-boyfriend. I wouldn't want him lying awake in bed all night wondering what *might* have taken place, when there was no reason to wonder at all.

"Oh, good! You needed a change of scenery to take your mind off things for a minute," he suggested.

"So, did you have a long day at the office," I asked, changing the subject.

"It was exhausting as hell. I was in one meeting after another to trying to come up with a plan on how we can increase our numbers next month." Charles yawned into the receiver.

"Excuse me, baby. I don't mean to be rude," he apologized.

"Go back to bed, sleepy head. I'll see you tomorrow evening. I'll sit in the cell phone lot until you call me, then I'll swing around to the arrival deck and scoop you up," I instructed.

"Alright, baby. Good night," he replied, yawning again before hanging up.

The ride back to Mama's house wasn't long, but the whole while, I thought about how lucky I was to have Charles. I'd been very skeptical about giving my heart completely to anyone up to this point, but I was beginning to feel a sense of safety with him and I missed him more than I ever imagined I could since I've been away from him these past few days.

When I turned the corner onto her street, Mama's house stood out like a beacon in the midst of a storm. There were four cars already in the driveway when I pulled in, but neither of them belonged to Bliss. Now I see why Mama was worried to death about her. I know I'd have a hard time falling asleep for trying to imagine what I'm going to say to her in the morning when she asks if I saw the show.

EIGHTEEN

"Hey, beauty queen! Mama wants to know if you're coming down for breakfast." Monica was dressed in shorts and a tee shirt and was lacing up a pair of Nikes.

"Why are you waking me so early," I complained.

"Uhhh. It's almost nine o' clock. Just how much beauty sleep do you need?" she teased.

"Where are you going?" I asked, sitting straight up in the bed.

"I'm going running after breakfast. Wanna go?" she asked.

"I'll pass on the running. But, tell Mama I'll be down in minute. I'm gonna freshen up first."

This was the first time since Tuesday that I felt sick to my stomach. As soon as I shut the bathroom door, I ran straight to the toilet to throw up. The smell of bacon frying was what set it off, but it didn't take long for me to get myself together.

Bonita had stayed overnight and Chauntel came over early to have breakfast with us. Monica and Veronica were also seated at the table.

"Where's Bliss?" I asked, hoping that she'd come home last night.

"Upstairs sleeping. She didn't get in till almost three this morning," Veronica answered.

"Yeah, she'll probably sleep until about noon, then she'll get up and get herself all prettied up, then she's off again for the rest of the day. It's like she just cannot stay home no matter what." Monica shook her head in disgust as she set the plates on the table.

Mama brought in eggs, bacon, fried potatoes, biscuits, and slices of fresh cantaloupe. I reached for a few slices of melon and put a spoonful of eggs on my plate.

"Is that all you're going to have?" Mama asked as she returned with a pitcher of orange juice.

"I'm trying to avoid heavy breakfasts. I want just enough to kick start my day, but not too much to where I'll be dragging my feet all morning," I replied.

"So, how was dinner last night? Did you ever meet up with your friend?" Mama asked.

"Yes, we had a good time catching up." I gave her the short version so that no one would start asking questions about who it was, what we did, and where we did it.

I kept checking the time as we ate and chatted about who planned to come to Granny's funeral and who didn't, as well as things that were left for us to do.

"Oh, just to let you know, someone from the printing company will drop off the programs for the funeral this evening. They're bringing them here," I said.

"Going somewhere?" Mama asked as I pushed back from the table.

"I have to run another errand this morning. Why, did you have plans for me?" I asked as I cleared my place at the table.

"I thought we'd take Papa over to Cunningham's to view the body and drop off the clothes Geri picked out for Granny, but I guess we can do it when you get back from your errand. Are you going to be long?" Mama asked.

"I should be back by noon," I answered, heading toward the stairs.

Although I dreaded it, I figured I'd better have a talk with Bliss this morning. I want her to know how I feel after seeing the show, so I tiptoed to her room and tapped lightly on the door. When I didn't get a reply, I peeped in to see if she was awake. She was in her bed facing the wall with the covers over her head.

"Bliss," I whispered.

"Are you awake?"

There was no reply, so I turned around to head back out.

"Don't leave, Bree," Bliss said from under the covers.

"I can't sleep." Bliss pulled the covers back and sat up in the bed, turning to face me.

"I came to tell you that I saw the show last night," I began.

"You did? I didn't even see you," she said.

"Look, Bliss. I know for myself that you're very good dancer. And dancing can possibly take you lots of places in your life, but I am very uncomfortable with the environment I was in last night watching your show. I'm even *more* uncomfortable knowing that you're there on your own when you're performing."

"Yeah, well I guess you don't have to be uncomfortable any more because I got fired last night after the show," she said.

"Fired? For what?" I asked

"Last night after the show, my manager, Pete, came to the dressing room asking if I wanted to triple my money for the night and of course I said yes. So, he tells me there are some people in the V.I.P. room who would pay top dollar for a private show. He promised it was safe, so I agreed. A couple of the customers started getting physical and when I complained to Pete about it, he told me to stop whining and grow up or get the hell out, so I left. He told me if I walked out the door I was fired, but I didn't know what else to do, so I left." Bliss looked at me as though she were waiting for my advice.

"Oh, my goodness! You see what I'm talking about? Did any one of them hurt you, because if they did," I didn't finish my sentence before Bliss cut in.

"They didn't have a chance to. I was scared as hell, so I got outta there fast," she said.

"Good! I hope you never go back there again, and you need to stay as far away from this Pete person as possible because he obviously doesn't care about you," I added.

"Yeah, I know. He proved that last night," she sighed.

"*Now* what am I gonna do for money? He didn't even pay me! All I have are my tips from the show."

"That's the last thing you need to worry about. You can look for a job, and in the meantime, I'll help you out. But I want you to promise me that you'll stay away from Pete *and* that club." I spoke sternly as I looked her directly in the eyes.

"Okay, I promise," she responded as she threw herself back onto the pillow and pulled the covers back over her head.

"Well, I'd better get dressed. I have an errand to run and then we're taking Papa to Cunningham's to view Granny's body and drop off her clothes. You wanna go with us?"

"If I'm up when you get back, maybe I'll go," she replied.

"I'll check on you when I get back," I said as I closed the door behind me and headed toward the bathroom at the end of the hall. The thought of a hot shower and my tropical scented body wash sounded better by the minute. If only it could wash all my problems away like it did the dirt off my body.

NINETEEN

By the time I'd finished dressing, it was almost ten thirty. I pulled my hair back and secured it with a clip in the back and grabbed my purse.

"I'm heading out, Mama. Be back in a little bit," I yelled out before closing the front door.

The ride to Attorney Simmons' office in Rock Hill was about twenty minutes from Mama's house. As I left the city limits behind, the office buildings and warehouses that lined the interstate disappeared and in an instant I was surrounded by beautiful, emerald green trees that danced in the morning breeze and welcomed those entering the Palmetto State.

I was able to trace my steps back to Attorney Simmons' office without any problems. When I walked into the office, the young receptionist stood to greet me from behind her desk.

Hmmm. That was awfully polite.

"I see you made it back this morning," she said.

"Yes. I would've been here sooner, but I slept a little later than usual this morning," I said as I looked around the office for Attorney Simmons.

"Oh, Attorney Simmons is with a client at the moment, but let me buzz him and let him know you're here," she said as she dialed his extension.

"Yes, sir. Mr. Baker's granddaughter is here," she said in a soft tone.

"Have a seat. He'll be right with you."

No sooner than I took a seat, Attorney Simmons walked out of his office with the same yellow envelope that I'd given to him yesterday. He motioned for me to follow him into a small conference room and closed the door behind us.

"Good morning, Miss Baker. Good to see you again," he said as he sat and opened the envelope.

"I'm sorry to interrupt your meeting. I could've waited," I said.

"No, that won't be necessary. I'll be with that client for a while and I want to go ahead and give you this. I actually just got back from the bank a short while before you arrived. They tried to give me problems with one of the checks. Your baby sister's information was incomplete, but I told them I wasn't leaving without all the checks.

Attorney Simmons proceeded to remove all the contents of the big yellow envelope and sorted through some papers until he found what he was looking for.

"Who, Bliss?" I asked.

"No. *Sonetta*," he replied as he handed me the data sheet.

In the date of birth section there was a clause that instructed to list the names of the mother and father if the person was a minor. There was no mother's name listed, but Daddy's name, Barnett Baker, Jr. was listed as the father. This had to be some kind of mistake.

As I continued to examine the paper, Attorney Simmons placed all but one small envelope back into the larger one. "Well, here you are, Miss Baker." He waved the smaller envelope in the air. "Tell Mr. Baker that something personal somehow made it into this envelope by accident, but I'm stuffing it back inside for him," he said as he stuffed the smaller envelope back inside. "Please give Mr. Baker my regards and tell him that I will see him at the service on Saturday." Attorney Simmons stood and shook my hand and asked the receptionist to see me out.

I was still stunned when I walked out of the conference room, and didn't really hear what the receptionist said as I left the office. I sat in my car for a few minutes trying to absorb everything that had just happened before I headed back to Mama's house, but nothing made sense. I couldn't help but wonder if Granny made a blatant error on the paper, or if Daddy truly was Sonetta's father. No matter what, I had to know the truth.

Oh God! What if I regret ever knowing?

It doesn't matter. At this point, I had no choice. I had to find out the truth about Sonetta or I'd never be able to rest. I wracked my brain as I tried to figure out where I could start to look for answers when it hit me.

The boxes at Granny's house!

I suddenly remembered the envelope marked *Sonetta* with the pictures of Granny in a hospital room holding a baby. Maybe that's Sonetta's mother. That envelope ought to have some clues.

What did I do with that envelope?

Thinking back to Tuesday night, I remembered suggesting to Papa that I put all the photos in the scrapbook box so that I can have Mama create one for him. I put the box marked *Scrapbook* in my trunk when

I left Papa's and never took it out, so as far as I know it's still there.

I was tempted to pull over on the interstate and go through the box, but I decided to wait until I got back to Mama's house. When I arrived, I grabbed the box out of the trunk and went inside.

"Bree, is that you?" I heard Mama ask from the family room.

"Yes. I'm going to run upstairs for a minute. I'll be right back down," I said as I ran upstairs and into Monica's room. Without hesitating, I sat on the bed and began rummaging through the box until I came across the white envelope marked *Sonetta.* There were three photos inside, all of Granny holding the baby with some other woman sitting near. On the back of one photo, the faded name *Deb* had been written in pencil.

Was that the name of the woman in the photos? Was she Sonetta's real mother?

My brain traveled a hundred miles an hour as I tried to piece things together, but still nothing made sense. This wasn't something I could bring to just anyone's attention unless I was sure. I usually had the answer to most things, but this time I was baffled. I couldn't just go to Mama asking questions – what if it was true and she never knew about it?

This Deb person is sure to show up at Granny's funeral, especially if Daddy is Sonetta's father.

I decided to be on the lookout for her at the funeral tomorrow and until I had some solid answers, I had to keep this information to myself.

Suddenly, I thought of the small envelope that Attorney Simmons said he found accidentally in big yellow envelope. I reached inside the big envelope and pulled out all the contents, in search of something that looked out of place. I found what appeared to be a letter from Granny that was addressed to Papa. It was sealed.

Perhaps this letter was the key to everything. Otherwise, why would it be in this envelope with the others? But, how could I read it without tearing the seal? I only had one choice if I wanted to know what was inside; I had to open it.

Careful not to tear the letter inside, I slid my finger under the flap of the envelope and slowly lifted the seal. Hesitating a moment from guilt, I reached inside and removed the letter, opening it slowly as I took several deep breaths.

January 1, 2008

My Dearest Barnett,

As we celebrate the New Year, I wanted to write the things that are on my heart. By the time you read this letter, I will have gone home to take my eternal rest. I've done all that was needed to leave something behind to my thirteen beautiful grandchildren, and I trust with my whole heart that you will take care of everything and everyone else as we'd planned. I'm so thankful to have shared such a wonderful life with you and I hope that when I'm gone you will treasure the memories we made together. I couldn't have asked for a better companion. We have carried this family through some tough times and even though I knew you didn't agree with the decision we made about Sonetta, I still feel it was for the best. Someday, I hope you will see it that way and that you won't hold it against Mayva or Geri for agreeing with me. Our son did the unthinkable, but he was still our son and we had to do whatever we could to hold our family together, even if it meant going as far as we did. I hate to leave you, but this old heart of mine won't last much longer. Always know that you were my gift from God. Take care of yourself, dear. And take care of our family.

Your devoted wife,
Beulah Mae

"Granny knew she was going to die and they never told us," I whispered softly as I wiped the tears from my eyes.

The letter that I'd just read clearly indicated that Mama and Aunt Geri were both aware of my father's indiscretion. It must have been terrible for Mama to find out that the man she'd loved and had twelve children with had been having an affair, and even worse that he'd had a child outside their marriage. I couldn't begin to imagine what she must've gone through, and to have kept all that pain bottled up inside for all these years must have been so hard for her.

Something Granny said in the letter struck me as odd. She said they had to do whatever they could to hold the family together, even if it meant going as far as they did. Was she referring to the adoption? What did they do – did they *force* Sonetta's mother to give her up? Whatever it was, I had to know, and I had to find out *before* I left to go back to Georgia.

I slid the pictures back into the small envelope and tucked it back into my purse for safe keeping. Since I was careful opening it, I was able to reseal Granny's letter to Papa, which I slid back into the big yellow envelope. I planned to return it to him today and prayed he wouldn't notice that I'd been inside.

As promised, I checked to see if Bliss was awake before leaving for Papa's house. She was still in bed with her head under the covers, and in light of what she went through last night at the club, I decided I wouldn't bother her.

Everyone waited for me outside by the car.

"Ready?" I asked as I hit the unlock button on the key fob.

"Let's go," Mama said as she climbed in the back seat with Chauntel.

Bonita jumped into the front passenger seat and we were off to Fort Mill once again.

TWENTY

We arrived at Papa's house just in time to see some of Granny's choir members leaving. Papa introduced them and said that they'd come over to see if there was anything they could do to help before the funeral.

"Sisters, we thank you so much for coming by and offering to help. I know that my wife will be smiling down tomorrow when you sing her favorite song, "*Peace Be Still,*" Papa said as he ushered them to their car.

"And we will be so happy to oblige, Brother Baker. You take care now and don't you forget to call if you need *anything* at all," the driver said before pulling out of the driveway.

"Papa, who's that woman driving?" Bonita asked as they drove down the street.

"Oh, that's Sister Ida Harvell. She's the director of the senior choir," he replied as we walked toward the house.

"Well, you beware of Sister Ida because she seems a little too eager to help," she warned.

Bonita was only kidding and we all laughed, but if the truth were told, Papa would be a fine catch for any older woman who was looking to land herself a good man. He was handsome, strong, considerate and a hard worker – as fine as they come. But Papa only had eyes for Granny, so Sister Ida and the crew had better look elsewhere for their golden opportunity.

"Are you ready to go to Cunningham's, Papa?" I asked as we entered the house.

"I guess now is as good a time as ever. Let me get my things," he replied.

"Sonetta!" Papa shouted.

"We're about to head over to the funeral home now, but you can stay if you want," he finished.

Sonetta emerged from the living room and for the first time, I took notice of how beautiful she really was. Her long, wavy hair was swept up into a pony tail that cascaded down her neck and rested softly on her shoulders. The blazing South Carolina sun had already started creating a bronze glow against her naturally golden skin, and her deep, dark eyes burned with intensity.

"Hello, Sonetta," I said, stepping forward to embrace her.

"Breanna!" She ran to meet me.

"You've grown so much since the last time I was home." I inspected her from head to toe, surprised at how very different she suddenly appeared in my eyes.

"Got any more of those hugs to go around?" Mama asked as she reached for Sonetta.

"Hi, Aunt Mayva. Hi, Bonita. Hi, Chauntel." Sonetta hugged everyone.

"So how are you spending your summer, Sonetta?" I asked, suddenly wanting to know more about this young girl who has brought so much mystery into my life in the blink of an eye.

"I'm going to cheerleading camp and I also have a list of books to read for school," she replied enthusiastically.

"You like to read?" I asked as I pulled a chair out from the kitchen table and took a seat.

"Yes. I'm on the avid readers program at school," she replied.

Before I could ask my next question, Papa had already returned carrying Granny's clothes.

"Y'all ready to get this over with?" he asked.

"Isn't Aunt Geri going?" I asked.

"No, she decided to stay home. She's not feeling up to this today."

"And I'm gonna stay here and watch television, Papa." Sonetta turned and headed back toward the living room.

"It was good to see you, Sonetta. I'll see you again later." I waved to her as we closed the door behind us.

After seeing Sonetta, I was even more determined to get to the bottom of things. The innocent slip of information by Attorney Simmons has piqued my interest to the point where I would not be satisfied until this had been settled in my mind.

I examined Mama's face on the way to the funeral home and couldn't help but wonder if she noticed my new interest in Sonetta back at the house.

The combination of my curiosity and the somber mood that seemed to spread like a disease throughout the car made the drive to the funeral home uneasy. I was happy to finally pull into the parking lot so that I could get out of this car. It was filled with gloom so thick you could cut it with a knife.

We were met at the door by the owner, J.P. Cunningham, who welcomed us into his office where we ironed out the plans for the service and burial. He assured Papa that everything would be handled with professionalism and the utmost care. When business concluded, Mr. Cunningham had a consultant escort us to the area where Granny's body was being prepared for the service.

My sisters and I broke down in tears when we saw Granny. To know that we'd never see or talk to her again was something we weren't prepared for. We held each other up during this difficult time, but I still had a sick feeling in my stomach. Granny was the glue that held our family together and the thought that we'd be left alone without her was unsettling, to say the least.

Mama and Papa remained strong as they discussed the grooming details. The clothing and instructions were given to the consultant who in turn reminded us of the plans for tomorrow's service, then led us to the door.

"You alright, Papa?" I asked as we walked to the car.

"I'm holding it together, baby girl," he replied with his head hung low.

I never would've imagined that Papa could be so strong after losing Granny. I worried that he held everything together in everyone's presence, but would fall apart when no one was around to help him.

"Why don't we go back to the house and I'll make us all some lunch," Mama suggested, trying to brighten the mood.

"That's the best thing I've heard all day," I added.

When we returned to Papa's house, Mama started making sandwiches and I put together a salad using lettuce from the fridge, and a tomato and cucumber that Papa had grown in the garden out back.

I checked the living room for Sonetta, but the television had been turned off and there was no sign of her. I'd hoped she would still be there so that she could join us for lunch and I could learn more about her.

Oh, well. I'll just catch up with her tomorrow.

Over lunch, we made plans to meet at Papa's house around ten o'clock in the morning. With the funeral starting at noon, we decided to play it safe in the event some showed up late. The cars from the funeral home were due to arrive at Papa's around eleven-thirty, and that's when the cars would begin their procession to the church.

Papa also asked that we have everyone meet back at his house immediately after the family repast for a meeting. I didn't ask, but it seemed obvious that he plans to distribute the checks from the money that Granny left us at that time.

When everyone had become restless, I suggested we head back to Mama's house. My body was screaming for sleep and I'd done all I could do to keep my eyes open to this point. I've reached the breaking point that my body has apparently developed over the last few weeks. At a certain time of day, no matter what's going on, I now had an uncompromising need to close my eyes.

Before we left, I whispered to Papa to meet me in the living room.

"Here's the envelope from Attorney Simmons' office. I picked it up this morning."

"Oh yeah! I almost forgot," Papa said as he opened the clasp and peeked inside.

"Looks like everything is final. I'll give these out tomorrow afternoon. Thanks for everything, baby girl," Papa said as he fastened the clasp on the envelope.

"Anything for you, Papa. Is there anything you need me to do before tomorrow?"

"I believe everything is under control. I'm expecting your Aunt Mary Jo and Uncle Ernest to come by later and Geri's coming back over in a little while, so we'll manage," he said.

"Alright. I'll see you tomorrow morning. Love you."

"I love you, too, Bree," he said as we headed back to the kitchen.

I decided not to mention that Attorney Simmons had found something personal in the envelope. I wanted to give the seal a chance to dry completely, and besides, Papa would find it whenever he was ready to disburse the checks to everyone.

Bonita and Chauntel were at the door waiting.

"C'mon, Bree. Mama said she'd meet us at the car. She went to check on Dee."

When I was finally outside the house I let out a sigh of relief. I'd been anticipating the trip to the funeral home and was glad that it was over and done with. As soon as we got back to Mama's house, I'd be heading straight upstairs to take a nap.

As we headed back to the city, I thought about seeing Charles later this evening and looked forward to being in his arms again. Safe.

TWENTY-ONE

I didn't waste any time getting to bed at Mama's house. With Monica out, I had the room to myself, which made it easier for me to fall asleep. The moment my head hit the pillow, I was out. It was obvious that I'd slept hard because it was nearly four hours later when I finally woke up.

Charles' plane wasn't due to land for another hour, but I decided to get up anyway. Being out in the heat all morning and afternoon had me feeling sweaty and I wanted to freshen up and change my clothes before picking him up.

I realized during my walk to the bathroom at the end of the hall that my naps were getting longer and whenever I woke up, it was harder for me to get up and around. It felt as though I carried a ton of bricks on my back and it seemed like the bathroom moved further away the longer I walked. If Mama experienced this feeling every time she became pregnant, I don't know what could've possibly possessed her to allow herself to become pregnant the next time.

When I'd finally gotten in the shower, I stood still under the pulsating spray for at least five minutes straight trying to fully wake up. After the fragrance of my tropical shower gel began to find its way into my nostrils, I came alive again. I never would've thought that in the middle of the day it would take this much effort to liven up, but I'd finally gotten into the groove of things once again.

I chose a simple, but classy summery dress to wear. With it being Friday and Charles coming to my home town, I decided I'd take him to dinner. Careful not to overdo it with the perfume, I applied a light coat of body cream and topped it off with a couple pumps of light spray. To compliment the dress, I slipped into a pair of open-toe heels and transferred the contents of my purse into one that matched my shoes. I checked around the room one last time to make sure I'd packed everything back into my bags before heading downstairs.

"Time to go already?" Mama asked as I walked into the family room where she and Bonita were watching an episode of *Law and Order*.

"Umph! Where are you going looking like *that*? I know that's not how you normally dress when you pick up someone from the airport," Bonita commented.

"Yes, Charles' plane lands in twenty-five minutes and no, I don't normally look like this when I go to the airport, but I thought I'd take Charles to dinner since he's in my home town," I said as I looked from Mama to Bonita.

"I'm going to bring Charles by to say hello before we go to dinner, so I'll see you guys in just a little while," I said as I headed to the foyer where my bags were waiting.

I took the scenic route to the airport so that I had time to relax and clear my thoughts. So much had taken place in the little time that I'd been in Charlotte – not to mention what I went through earlier this week after learning of my pregnancy. I could still hear Dr. McGhee's words echoing in my mind.

Breanna, the test results are positive; you're five weeks pregnant.

How much can one person take?

I thought the scenic route would help me clear my head, but I was obviously mistaken. All it did was allow the time and space needed for me to bring everything I was facing to the forefront of my mind. Before I realized it, I found myself turning into Douglas International Airport and looking for a shaded space in the cell phone lot where I could park to wait for Charles to call and let me know when his plane landed. There was a spot under some overhanging trees where I pulled in and popped in a jazz CD and closed my eyes, hoping to relax for the next ten minutes.

I jumped in my seat when my mobile phone rang at twelve minutes after seven. I'd apparently dozed off to sleep while listening to music.

"Hello." I placed my hand on my chest and tried to calm down from being startled.

"Touchdown, baby! I can't wait to see you," Charles said with excitement.

"Me, too! I'm in the cell phone lot. Do you have to go to baggage claim?" I asked.

"No. I carried my luggage on board with me. I'm still on the concourse now – walking past all the gates. And as luck would have it, mine was at the very end." Charles let out a long sigh.

"Well, I'll wait another ten minutes before heading to the arrival deck. See you then," I said, trying to remain calm.

"Alright, babe. See you in a few." Charles hung up.

Using the rearview mirror, I checked my hair and touched up my lip gloss. I want Charles to smile when he saw me, and although I was sure to catch his eye in this dress, he'd feel the same way if I came to pick him up wearing a tee shirt and sweat pants. He has always made me feel beautiful, no matter what I was wearing.

When the time came, I left the cell phone lot and headed toward the arrival deck. I spotted Charles on the curb about halfway down and pulled over with my flashers blinking.

He looked perfect in his jeans with a casual shirt and shoes. He smiled and dropped his bags as I got out of the car and threw his arms around me.

"Baby!" he whispered in my ear as he held me tight.

With my eyes closed and my arms tightly around him, we were suspended in time. Charles leaned down and kissed my lips and in my mind I was home again.

We put the bags in the trunk and got in.

"So, how was your flight?" I asked as I was about to pull off from the curb.

Before I could change gears, Charles had pulled my face to his and we were locked in a passionate kiss.

"Charles. The people," I started.

"I don't care, Bree. You have no idea how much I've missed you," he said as he kissed me over and over again.

"Yes I do, baby, because I've missed you just the same." I gave in and welcomed him to Charlotte with the sweetest kiss before finally pulling off from the curb and exiting the airport.

"So where are we headed?" Charles asked as he played with the hair on my neck.

"Well, I thought I'd take you by the house first to see my mother and then I'm taking you to dinner!" I announced.

"You are? That's so sweet of you, baby. Oh, by the way, I've made reservations for us tonight and tomorrow at the Hyatt Place. Do you know where this is?" Charles asked as he pointed to a map on the Google directions he'd printed out.

I quickly glanced at the map.

"I know the area. We'll find it," I replied.

Charles put the map into the glove compartment and grabbed my hand as he enjoyed the view from the car. When we pulled up to Mama's house there were several cars already there.

"What's going on? Who do all these cars belong to?" Charles asked as we found a spot on the curb.

"Looks like my brothers and sisters are here," I replied with excitement. I hadn't seen any of my brothers since I've been home.

"Uh oh. Here we go," Charles said sarcastically as we went into the house.

"You'll be fine, silly," I replied, tapping him playfully on his hand.

"Is this a coincidence or what?" I asked as we walked into the family room where everyone gathered.

"Bree!" My brother BJ jumped up from the sofa and hugged me.

"Y'all remember Charles, right?" I asked.

"Oh, yeah! Good to see you again, Charles," BJ said as he and Charles shook hands.

Everyone hugged each other. I was excited to see my brothers Dante, Joey, and Kory and my sister, Joy, for the first time since I was home during the holidays. My sisters-in-law and brothers-in-law were also there, and my nieces and nephews played with each other while the adults chatted.

"Drinks anyone?" Bliss came into the family room carrying a few six-packs of soda.

"I'm getting hungry. What about you?" I asked Charles as he listened to my oldest brother BJ tell about his latest adventure as a UPS Driver.

"I could eat," he replied.

"Mama, we're gonna get ready to go," I said as Charles and I stood to leave.

"Wait! Before anyone leaves I have an announcement to make. We're all expected to meet at Papa's house tomorrow morning at ten o'clock in the morning. Everyone! No exceptions!" Mama stood in the middle of the living room and looked at everyone to make sure they understood.

"We'll be there," I said as we walked to the door.

"Bree, where are you and Charles staying?" Mama asked as she escorted us to the door.

"The Hyatt Place. But if you need me, just call the mobile. It'll be on," I replied.

"Alright. Charles, you take care of my little girl." Mama hugged Charles and kissed me on my forehead.

"Yes, ma'am. I will." He grabbed my hand as we walked to the car.

"You heard your mother; she told me to take care of you. I think she likes me," he said, while opening the driver side door.

"I'm driving tonight," I said as I climbed into the driver seat.

"And yes, my mother loves you," I added with a smile.

"Good! What's for dinner?" Charles asked as he walked around to the passenger side.

“I’m taking you to a quiet little Italian restaurant over in Dilworth. You’ll love it,” I replied.

My man and I were together again, and for the time being, I’d forgotten all about everything that has plagued my mind for the past few days. Everything was all good.

TWENTY-TWO

We were lucky to get an intimate booth in the corner of the restaurant that had a view of the fountain outside. We enjoyed the authentic Italian cuisine and the ambiance of the serene setting, which became an aphrodisiac as the night went on.

"Thanks for dinner, baby," Charles said as he motioned for the waiter.

"Did you save room for the Tiramisu?" the waiter asked as he held out a dessert menu.

"We'll take one Tiramisu to go," Charles said as he kept his eyes on mine.

One look and I knew what he was thinking. When Charles was feeling intimate, he became very serious and his eyes spoke for him. I couldn't say that I didn't feel the same. After all, we'd been sharing the same bed for the past six months and our bodies had practically become one. Being away from him these last few days has increased my appetite for him and I couldn't wait until we were finally alone.

As planned, I took care of the bill and we headed to our hotel for the night. I let the car windows down so that we could soak up the night's summer breeze which made its way into the car as we drove. The jazzy sound of the saxophone wrapped itself around us as it echoed from the speakers, and the moon glowed full and stood prominent against the night sky. This night was perfect. Nothing that happened before this moment mattered - at least not tonight.

Charles parked the car and took care of our bags as I checked in at the front desk. Looking around, I noticed that the décor of the hotel was in perfect alignment with the mood we'd set for the night. We were given a suite in a quiet corner on the third floor and as I opened the door, Charles stopped me just before entering.

"Wait! Wait! Wait! Stand right there, Bree. I wanna do this the right way," he said as he slid past me and placed the bags inside the room.

Charles came back out, picked me up, and carried me into the room. He closed the door with his foot, secured it with the deadbolt, then carried me over to the king size bed and lay me down gracefully. I watched as he slowly undressed. First he removed his shoes, then his jeans and shirt, and finally his boxer briefs. I lay there marveling at his statuesque body, wanting it against mine. As Charles lay next to me, he softly moved my hair from the back of my neck and unzipped my dress. One shoulder at a time, he removed the dress, the bra, and finally my panties, and I lay naked in the middle of the bed as the light from the moon that peeked in between the small opening in the drapes glowed directly upon my breast.

Charles kissed and explored every inch of my body with his tongue. He made me feel as though he loved all of me – not just a part of me, but every part. His heavy breathing against my neck created a fire deep down in my core and I begged for him to be inside me.

"Charles, please," I pleaded with my head tilted back as he teased.

"Tell me you missed me," he commanded as he stroked and kissed my neck.

"I missed you, Charles. I missed you so much," I obeyed.

"I love you, Breanna, with all that I am," he said.

I gasped as I tightened my grip around his neck and my legs around his waist while Charles made love to my body and my mind until we were both exhausted and weakened from passion.

Charles fell asleep as I stroked his chest with my fingertips.

This man loves me.

I couldn't deny Charles' love for me, but could it be enough? Would it be enough? Linden loved me once, also, but when the time came for him to prove his love, it wasn't enough. *I* wasn't enough. How could I be sure that Charles wouldn't do the same?

Rather than suffer through another disappointment, I'd just make sure there wasn't a chance for that to happen. Anyway, this was an accident. I never intended to get pregnant and there was no reason Charles should have to suffer because of it.

I'd convinced myself that terminating the pregnancy was the right thing to do; that it wasn't the right time for a baby. But no matter what, the thought of it got under my skin. The question of how I would live with the guilt kept coming back up in my mind. I couldn't sleep from the torture; I had to call Camilla.

"Where you going, baby?" Charles asked as I got out of bed and went into the other room to get my mobile phone.

"I can't sleep so I'm gonna watch a movie in the other room," I said.

"You want me to come in there with you?" he asked.

"No, go back to sleep, baby. I'll come back to bed in a little while," I replied as I turned on the television in the living area.

I dialed Camilla's mobile number.

"What's up, Bree? Aren't you with Charles?" she asked.

"Mill." I could only get one word out before she started in on me.

"Uh oh, what's wrong? Did y'all fall out? What did you do, Bree?"

"What are you talking about? I didn't do anything," I whispered.

"Okay, let's start over. How's everything going? Are you okay?" she asked, sounding like a kindergarten teacher.

"I'm fine. I'm just in my feelings tonight, that's all," I replied, trying to turn our conversation into a serious one.

"Well, are you going to tell me what happened?" she asked.

"Everything was fine for a while. I picked Charles up from the airport and took him back to the house to see my family. Then, I took him out to dinner and the mood was set and we got to the hotel and made love, and now I'm feeling bad because I can't stop thinking about… well, you know."

"This is just the reason why you can't go through with it, Bree! This thing is going to haunt you until…"

I cut her off in mid sentence.

"I need your support, no matter what I decide. Can you do that? Please?" I pleaded.

"You have my support, Bree. But I just have one thing to say and then I'm shutting up."

"What's that?" I asked, frustrated.

"Charles *loves* you, Bree! I feel it with every fiber of my being! He is *not* going to abandon you! He's not Linden. Do you hear me?" Camilla became completely silent.

"I hear you," I replied and changed the subject.

"So what time did you get in?" I asked after taking a deep breath.

"Nine. Mom picked me up and we went for a glass of wine. I'm just getting settled in at her place," she replied.

"I haven't seen her in a while. Will she be with you at the funeral tomorrow?" I asked.

"Yep. She's coming. So what time should I be there?" she asked.

"Twelve sharp. Trinity Baptist in Fort Mill. Do you think you'll have any problems finding it?" I asked.

"I'll get directions from the internet." Camilla yawned into the phone.

"Now, *that* was rude!" I complained.

"Sorry. I'm pooped! And shouldn't *you* be asleep? You've got a long day ahead of you tomorrow," she implied.

"That's all I've been doing – sleeping! I'm gonna stay up and watch a movie until I get sleepy. I'll see you tomorrow. Thanks, Camilla."

"Anytime, honey. See you tomorrow," she said as she disconnected the call.

I lay back against the cushion on the L-shaped sofa and rested my feet on the ottoman. Camilla's words rang in my head and I was flooded with thoughts of everything from Granny's funeral to the news about Sonetta. Suddenly, everything was a ball of confusion all over again and I looked forward to this weekend being over. I hoped to uncover the truth about Sonetta tomorrow, so that when I left Charlotte, I wouldn't be leaving any loose ends.

I hit the power button on the remote control and the plasma television lit up. While surfing through the channels, I came across a movie starring Martin Lawrence that I hadn't seen. If anything can make me crack a smile, it was Martin, so I settled on the sofa and laughed until I'd fallen asleep.

In the middle of the night, Charles came into the living room and carried me to the bed, where he tucked me under the sheets and held me as we both slept through the rest of the night.

TWENTY-THREE

"Rise and shine, beautiful," Charles said as he opened the drapes.

I squinted from the sudden burst of sunlight in my face.

"What time is it?" I asked, pulling the covers over my face.

"It's eight o'clock. I went downstairs and got us some breakfast." Charles arranged the tray of food on the desk in the living area.

"I'm not hungry," I said as I turned over in the bed.

"Well, you have to have *something,* Bree! You're gonna need your energy for today, so let's go," he said as he pulled the covers from over my head and forced me out of bed.

I slipped into one of Charles' tee shirts and went over to the vanity to wash my face.

Charles had gone downstairs and gotten two bagels with cream cheese, fruit, juice, and coffee from the complimentary breakfast bar. I ate a bagel and a banana, and drank some coffee.

"Feeling better?" Charles asked as he took the last bite of his bagel.

"A little. What I need is a shower," I replied as I got up to get my toiletry bag.

"Why don't you go on ahead of me. I'm going to touch up my clothes and make sure I don't have any wrinkles," Charles suggested.

"Ooh! Would you mind touching up my dress when you're done? It's in my garment bag," I said, pointing to the bag.

"No problem."

"Speaking of bags, have you seen my laptop?" I asked as I looked around the room.

"No, and it wasn't in the trunk when I got the bags out," he replied.

"When was the last time you saw it?" he asked.

"I used it at Mama's house Thursday morning to make the programs for the funeral. I must've left it in Monica's room. I'll get it before I leave," I said.

"See you in a few," he said as I headed into the bathroom.

As I showered, I thought about Papa and hoped that he was okay. Today, he will bury the woman he shared his life with for the past fifty-five years. That had to be weighing down heavily on his heart. I suddenly wanted to hurry and get dressed so that we could get going to Papa's house in case he needed help with something.

I called out to Charles when I finished showering to ask if he wanted me to leave the water running.

"I'm on my way," he said.

When he went in, I quickly rubbed myself down in scented body cream and touched up my face and hair. By the time Charles was finished with his shower, I had gotten as far as my underclothes and pantyhose.

"Wow! You're moving fast!" he said as he quickly dried himself off with the towel.

"I started thinking about Papa when I was in the shower and I thought he might need my help with something. I just want to hurry and get over there," I said as I slipped into my sleeveless black dress.

"Well, let me catch up. Will you get my socks and shoes out of the duffle bag?" he asked.

"I love seeing you in a suit and tie. You look so distinguished," I said as I helped with the cuffs on his shirt.

"If you think I look good in a suit, you should see me in a tuxedo!" He was being sarcastic.

"Maybe one day I will," I replied nonchalantly.

When Charles and I were fully dressed, we tidied up the room a bit and headed downstairs. I decided I'd drive since we were in a hurry. On the way to Fort Mill, Charles opened a new package of handkerchiefs and slid two in my purse. He put the third one in the inside pocket of his suit jacket.

"One for you and one for emergencies," he said.

"You've thought of everything, haven't you? Thank you so much for being here, Charles," I said, squeezing his hand.

"I told your mother I would take care of you, right?" he said as he smiled and looked out of the passenger window.

Within minutes, we had crossed over into South Carolina and were nearing the Fort Mill exit from the interstate. When I got closer to Papa's house, I could see that we were one of the first cars to arrive.

"It's only nine forty-five. Mama told everyone to be here at ten," I said, looking at my watch.

"Someone's already here," Charles said as a car approached.

It was Aunt Mary Jo and Uncle Ernest. Charles and I parked and walked to their car to meet them.

"Hi, Aunt Mary Jo. Uncle Ernest." I greeted them both with a hug.

"Hi, Baby! You're one of Barnett and Mayva's girls, aren't you?" she asked.

"Yes, ma'am. I'm Breanna and this is my boyfriend, Charles," I replied as Charles shook both their hands.

We didn't get to see Granny's sister and brothers often. Every few years we might see them at a reunion, but it wasn't often enough for them to remember the names and faces of twelve children. But I'd never forget Aunt Mary Jo. She and Granny looked a lot alike. The only difference what that Granny was a little taller and a little lighter than her sister. Otherwise, they could've been twins.

"We just got here and were about to go inside. You guys ready to go in?" I asked.

"Lead the way." Uncle Ernest smiled.

We went inside to find Papa fully dressed and sitting in his chair in the living room having a cup of coffee.

"Good morning, Papa. You remember Charles." Charles went over to Papa's chair.

"Mr. Baker. It's good to see you again. I'm sorry it had to be under these circumstances, but I came to support Breanna. She really loved her grandmother," he said as he shook Papa's hand.

"Thank you for coming, Charles. It's good to see you again also."

Aunt Mary Jo and Uncle Ernest came in behind us and took a seat on the sofa.

"Is there anything you need me to do, Barnie?" Aunt Mary Jo asked.

It was very rare that I heard Papa referred to as Barnie, but I guess Barnett *does* sound extremely formal.

"No, thank you. Everything is under control," he replied.

"Bree, you might want to go check on your sister," he suggested.

"Come on, Charles." I led the way down the hall toward Dee's room.

I tapped lightly on Dee's door before peeking in to see if she was dressed. When I saw that she was, I opened the door and went in. Dee was sitting in her chair, half facing the window and half facing the television as usual, watching CNN. She had on a black dress and shoes and her hair was pulled back into a ponytail. I walked over to her and put my hand on her shoulder.

"Hi, Dee. I'm back. And look who's here with me! You remember Charles," I said.

Charles walked over to where I was standing and placed his hand on top of Dee's on the armrest of the chair. Normally, Dee didn't take too well to strangers, but she didn't react at all to Charles touching her. She just kept rocking and watching CNN.

"Hello, Dee. It's good to see you again," he said in a soft tone.

"Well, I just wanted to come back and say hello – see if you needed help with anything. We'll be up front if you need me," I said as Charles and I left quietly.

"That's scary," Charles said as we walked down the hall toward the kitchen,

"What's scary?" I asked.

"To see a carbon copy of the woman I love," he replied.

Mama and Bonita were already in the kitchen and it seemed as though more of my brothers and sisters were arriving by the minute, or had called to say they were on their way.

The last to arrive was Bliss. She came rushing into the house like the drama queen that she was, ranting and raving about how her nail appointment was supposed to be at eight, but the technician didn't show up until almost nine o'clock. God forbid she should have to go through this day with a week-old manicure. What a disaster that would be!

I did a quick check in the living room, the kitchen, and outside to make sure that everyone was accounted for. I caught a glimpse of Granny's brothers, Uncle Jessie and Uncle Howard, in the living room, whom I hadn't seen in a couple years or more. Even though it was a sad occasion, it was good to see all the people together who loved Granny so much.

By the time the cars arrived from the funeral home, we were all outside and ready to start the procession to the church. There were four family cars following the Hearse, and a host of other cars following them. Charles and I were in the second family car with some of my brothers and sisters. Papa, Mama, and Granny's sister and brothers rode in the first car with their spouses.

We arrived at the church about ten minutes before noon. The funeral director arranged everyone in front of the church and prepared us for the family processional inside. When the drivers pulled the casket from the back of the Hearse, my heart dropped and my knees buckled under me. Charles grabbed me before I could fall.

"Breanna, are you okay?" he asked, pulling me up and laying my head on his chest.

"Oh, Charles. I don't know if I can take this." I trembled as I tried to hide the tears from the rest of my family.

Mama came over to see if I was okay.

"She became upset when she saw the casket being taken out. I've got her," he responded.

"Well, alright. Just let me know if you need me, Charles," Mama instructed.

"I will, ma'am," he responded as he held me while the Pallbearers took the casket inside the church.

"Charles, don't leave me alone," I said.

"I'm here, baby. I'm not going anywhere," he promised.

TWENTY-FOUR

The church was filled to capacity with standing room only. It was amazing to see how many people loved Granny. Everyone stood and the senior choir sang a beautiful selection as the family came down the middle aisle and were seated to the right. Our family was so large that we took up almost the entire right side of the church.

"Are you alright, Bree?" Charles asked as we took our seats.

"Yes," I replied, dabbing my eyes with the handkerchief he'd stuffed into my purse on the way to Papa's house this morning.

The service began with a beautiful prayer by the pastor, Reverend Armstrong. When he finished, he introduced the senior choir who performed a soul-stirring rendition of Granny's favorite song, *Peace Be Still.* I was so moved that I found myself standing and singing along with the choir. Other members of my family began standing, and eventually, the whole congregation was swaying and singing along. When it was time for Aunt Mary Jo to sing *Amazing Grace*, the church was already worked up and she was met with the same reaction.

Granny's home going service was just the way she would've wanted it to be. It was filled with love and high praises which echoed throughout the sanctuary. Just as I'd imagined he would, Papa broke down when they opened the casket for the final viewing of Granny's body. The thought of never seeing her again was unimaginable, but Mama was by his side along with Granny's brothers and sister. They helped comfort him as he cried through the viewing.

My eyes were fixed on the women who came down the aisle to view Granny's body. I hadn't forgotten about the woman, Deb, in the picture, who might be Sonetta's birth mother. Although the picture was taken fourteen years ago, I looked for anyone who remotely resembled her. There were a few women that I saw who I planned to talk to after the service to see if I could get any information. Hopefully, they'd show up at the burial.

When the service ended, we loaded up the cars and went directly to Evergreen Cemetery, where Granny would be buried. Everything seemed to move so fast by this time. The funeral director didn't waste any time. As soon as the family had arrived and gathered around the site, Reverend Armstrong prayed and it was over. We lay flowers on the casket and were ushered back to our cars so that Granny could be buried.

While we were there, I managed to casually approach a couple women who I suspected could be the woman in the picture, but neither of them were Deb. They either knew Granny from church, or their parents were friends of hers or Papa's. I wasn't having any luck finding her, but I wasn't giving up. Perhaps I'd have better luck back at the church for the repast.

When we arrived, there were still quite a few people socializing and waiting to greet the family. Camilla and her mother made their way through the crowd and over to the table where Charles and I were seated.

"Camilla! Mrs. Sanders! Thank y'all for coming. It means so much to my family." I rose from the table to give them both a hug.

"You know I had to be here, Bree. How's everyone doing? How's Papa?" Camilla asked.

"As good as can be expected, but I think he'll be alright. He's sitting at that table with Mama and Granny's brothers and sister. Why don't you go over and let him know you're here. I'm sure he'd love to see you," I said as I pointed to their table.

"Oh, I see him. Listen, I'll talk to you later, Bree. I'll call you tomorrow," she said as she headed to Papa's table.

"Take care, Bree. It was good seeing you." Mrs. Sanders waved and followed Camilla through the crowd.

While Charles was busy talking with my brothers Joey and Dante, I decided to do a little detective work, but came up empty every time. I started to believe that I'd never find this woman – at least not today. Charles and I had planned to head back to Georgia tomorrow, so I began to panic.

There's just no way I can leave Charlotte without knowing the truth about Sonetta.

I made my way back over to the table where Charles was seated just in time to come face to face with Linden.

"I've been looking all over for you, Breanna. It was a beautiful service," he remarked as he grabbed my hand in his.

"Thank you for coming. My family is grateful," I replied nervously.

"So, who's your friend?" Linden asked, reaching out to shake Charles' hand.

Charles rose from his seat.

"This is my boyfriend, Charles. Charles, this is Linden," I replied.

"Linden. Well, Breanna has told me a lot about you," Charles said with confidence as he placed his arm around my waist.

My brothers looked at each other and smiled, then resumed their conversation.

"She has?" Linden asked as though he were shocked.

"Yes. It's a pleasure to finally meet you," Charles replied.

"You're a lucky man, Charles," Linden commented.

"Don't I know it." Charles looked at me as if to confirm Linden's comment.

"We're both very lucky," I added as I put my arm around Charles.

After a brief moment of silence, Linden cleared his throat.

"Well, it was good seeing you again, Breanna. Charles, you take care of her."

"I will."

"Thanks again for coming, Linden. Take care of yourself." I patted him on the hand and watched as he disappeared into the crowd.

When I sat back down, Charles leaned over and kissed my lips.

"What was that for?" I asked, smiling.

"That was for love," he replied.

The church volunteers brought plates of food and drinks over to our table. I didn't have much of an appetite, so I just picked over my food. I was quite thirsty, however, and ended up drinking two glasses of iced tea.

"You're not eating, Bree. Remember, you have to have *something* to maintain your energy," Charles scolded.

"Yes, oh healthy one!" I teased as I took a bite of the dinner role on my plate.

"Ha. Ha. Very Funny! Can you at least eat a forkful of vegetables or a bite of your chicken?" he pleaded.

"If you say so," I said as I put a forkful of green beans in my mouth.

Mama came over to the table and reminded everyone that immediately after eating, we were to go straight to Papa's house for a family meeting.

"Bree, I'm going to meet y'all over there. I feel like my pressure is up and I don't have any of my medication with me," Mama said as she placed her hand on her temple.

"Why don't you let me drive you, Mama," I suggested.

"Charles, I'm going home with my mother for a minute. Would you mind riding to Papa's house with Dante and I'll just meet you over there?" I asked.

"No problem. Is everything okay?" he asked.

"Yes. She just needs to go home and take her blood pressure medication. I'm going to drive her," I replied, grabbing my purse.

"Here. You might need to move the car or something," I said, handing Charles the car keys.

"Okay. I'll see you in a little while," he said, looking worried.

Mama and I stopped at the other tables on the way out to remind the others to go directly to Papa's house for a meeting after they finished eating. On the way to home, she talked about the funeral and all the people that came to pay their respects. While she talked, I thought of ways to get answers to the questions I had about Daddy's affair with Sonetta's mother. How long did the affair last? Where did she come from, and where is she now? And, was she forced to give Sonetta up for adoption? With nothing left to go on, I decided that I'd bring it up to Mama when we get home and see what she had to say about it. I had to know.

TWENTY-FIVE

When we arrived at the house, Mama went straight to the family room to look for her blood pressure pills and I followed behind her. We looked all over for them, and finally found the bottle stuffed between the cushions of the sofa.

"Whew!" Mama blew out a breath of relief.

"I don't know what I would've done without these," she said as she opened the bottle and took out a pill.

I decided if I was ever going to ask any questions, now was as good a time as ever, so I opened my mouth and let the words come out.

"Mama, what do you know about Sonetta's mother?" I asked.

She stood still.

"What do you mean *know* anything about her?" She answered my question with another question.

"Well, like who she is and where she is now." "Everyone knows that your Aunt Geri and Uncle Bill adopted her at birth. Why do you ask?"

"She's getting older and I just thought maybe the question of who her real parents were had come up in a conversation or something. I guess I just wanted to know more about her," I said, hoping Mama would admit to knowing the truth.

"I need a glass of water to take my pill," Mama said, changing the subject as she left the family room and headed for the kitchen.

I wasn't getting anywhere with this line of questioning, so I reached in my purse and pulled out the envelope marked *Sonetta.* I took the three photos out and held them in front of Mama.

"Did you know that Granny knew Sonetta's birth parents?" I asked.

Where did you get those?" Mama asked, glaring at the pictures as though she were just struck by bittersweet memories.

"I found them when I was going through Granny's boxes at Papa's house. Who is this woman, Mama?" I asked.

"I don't know her, Bree."

"Are you sure? Look at the back of the picture. Her name is Deb, Mama. Did Daddy have an affair with her?" I asked, becoming frustrated.

"Bree, there are some things that should be left where they are. Don't go digging into the past. Sometimes, it's best to let sleeping dogs lie." Mama said as she turned to me.

"Oh, really? So, we have secrets, Mama?" I asked as I slammed the photos on the kitchen counter.

"Let's talk about *your* secrets for a minute, Bree!" she snapped.

"*My* secrets? What are you talking about, Mama? I'm not keeping any secrets," I said.

"Oh, really? Let's see. I've had twelve children of my own, so you'd think I'd know a pregnant woman when I see one!" she yelled.

My eyes opened wide and my mouth fell open.

"Pregnant? What makes you think I'm pregnant?" I looked away.

"Look at me, Bree! The long naps every afternoon! That's not like you. Even Papa could see the glow on your face the first time he saw you this week."

I was speechless.

"Does Charles know?" she asked.

I looked away.

"Breanna Elaine Baker! You haven't told him? What are you planning to do, Bree?" She grabbed my shoulders, forcing me to look at her, but I turned away.

"No, Bree! Think about what you're doing," she pleaded.

"Mama, I didn't come here to talk about me," I said, cutting her off.

I pointed to the pictures on the counter.

"I want to know if Sonetta is my sister and I want to know who this Deb woman is." I shook my head. "I'm going to run upstairs to get my laptop and when I get back, we'll finish this conversation."

"Breanna, " Mama started.

"Mama, if Daddy had an affair, all you have to do is say so. I'm not going to be angry with *you,*" I assured her.

"I'll be right back." I sighed as I turned and headed toward the stairs.

Now where did Monica put my laptop?

I looked all around the room until I finally spotted my laptop case on the floor sticking out between the foot of the bed and the chest. Then I looked up and was suddenly frozen in my tracks.

I trembled.

No! It can't be!

There, hanging from the footboard were the two monogrammed throws that Mama made for Dee and me when we were kids.

BEB.

Breanna Elaine Baker.

DEB.

Deanna Elizabeth Baker.

I walked over to the bed and picked up Deanna's throw and stared at the initials, DEB. I walked around to the side of the bed and slid to the floor. Scenes from the past suddenly appeared from my memory. The way Dee had changed, the night of Daddy's accident and how Mama became so depressed afterwards.

For a moment, I was speechless as I cried and rocked back and forth on the floor, holding the throw in my arms. Then, suddenly from the pit of my stomach, there came a sound.

I screamed.

"Mama!" I screamed her name over and over again until she burst through the door.

"What in the world is going on?" she began, until she saw the initials on the throw that I held out to her.

"Oh, my God!" She kept saying those words over and over again.

Mama sat down on the floor next to me and put her arms around me.

"I never wanted you to know," she sobbed. "I'm so sorry, Bree. I never wanted you to know."

"So there *is* no Deb? There never *was* an affair? What happened, Mama? What happened?" I asked, crying uncontrollably.

"I don't know, Bree. Only Deanna knows and she locked it deep inside her a long time ago."

"And Daddy's fall…was it an accident, Mama?" I asked, afraid of what the answer might be.

"Yes, it was an accident! Your father was drinking that night and I saw something that didn't set quite right with me, and when I approached him about it we had an argument. He got nervous, then became angry and lost his balance at the top of the stairs," she cried. "He never admitted anything, but he didn't have to." Mama wiped her eyes.

"Who is the woman in the pictures? The one with Granny?"

"She's just the woman who arranged the adoption, Bree."

"And Sonetta?" I asked.

"She's Deanna's. She had her while she was away," Mama said as she looked away.

"What about Daddy?" I asked as I struggled between feelings of hurt and anger.

"Granny confirmed it after Sonetta was born. She took one look at her and she knew. The five of us sat down and talked, and we decided that Geri and Bill would adopt Sonetta and take care of her, and we would never bring it up again." Tears rolled down her cheeks and neck as she laid her head back against the bed and closed her eyes.

"Bree, I'm so sorry you had to find out this way. I never wanted you to know," she cried.

"What am I supposed to do now, Mama? What do I do?" I held my chest as I cried.

"You have to forget what you learned about Sonetta. It'll destroy our family and Granny would turn over in her grave if that happened. And you have to tell Charles about the baby," she said.

"Bree, you've been through so much. Don't you think it's time *you* are happy?" She asked.

"I'm scared, Mama," I admitted.

"Scared of what? Scared you're going to feel guilty about being happy? Bree, you have to move on. Dee is being taken care of. Sonetta's happy and she has a good home. I'm going to be okay. But what about you?" Mama moved the hair that covered my eyes.

"Do you love Charles?" She asked.

"Yes. I love him," I replied.

"Do you believe that he loves you?"

"I know he does, Mama. He's such a good man," I said as I took a deep breath.

"Bree, you've got to break this cycle of depression in our family. You can't do anything to change the past, but you *can* do something about your future. You have to decide right here. Right now. It's up to you, Bree." Mama put her arms around me and held me a few moments longer.

"Mama, I can't see anyone right now. Will you call Papa and make up *something*? And tell Charles that you dropped me off at the hotel and to meet me there when he's ready."

"You ready to go now?" she asked as she helped me up from the floor.

"Yes."

"Come on. People are going to start wondering where we are," she said.

Still sobbing, I folded the monogrammed throw and neatly hung it back across the footboard. Mama picked up my laptop and my purse, and helped me down the stairs. On the way to the hotel, she called Papa's house and told him that she wasn't able to find her blood pressure medicine, so we had to call in an emergency refill and wait for it at the pharmacy. She also told Papa to tell Charles to meet me at the hotel and that we'd be over to see him before I left to go back to Georgia tomorrow.

Mama pulled into a parking space at the hotel and turned off the engine. She walked me upstairs to make sure that I was safe in my room before heading back home.

"Here's your laptop." She smiled and sat it on the desk in the living area.

"Bree, you have a brand new life growing inside of you. A part of you and a part of Charles. Look around you – it's a *miracle*! It's a *good* thing! This is God's gift to you, baby," she said as she wrapped her arms around me.

"I love you, Mama," I said, squeezing her tight.

"I love you, too, my baby girl," she said as she kissed her hand and placed it on my stomach.

"Are you going to be alright alone until Charles arrives?" Mama asked.

"I'll be fine," I nodded.

"We're planning to leave tomorrow after we checkout, but I'll come by the house first," I said as Mama walked down the hall toward the elevator.

"Alright. I'll see you tomorrow."

When the elevator door closed, I went back inside and sat on the sofa. I knew Charles would be here soon, and he'd take one look at me and know that I'd been crying. After changing into a pair of boxers and a tank top, I tried to tone down some of the swelling from crying by rinsing my face with cold water, but it was useless. Only time could erase this painted on mask that I'd worn for so long. And time begins now.

TWENTY-SIX

When I heard the knock at the door, I took a deep breath.

"Who is it?"

"It's me, Bree."

I opened the door to find Charles standing there, looking totally confused. He didn't utter a word. He just came into the room, emptied his pockets, and began to undress. I sat on the sofa quietly, looking at the floor as he slipped into a pair of lounge pants and a tank top. I know he must be thinking that I was insane or that something really weird was going on. I disappeared with my mother after the burial and told him I'd meet him at my family meeting, but I never showed up and ended up here at the hotel looking as though I've been beaten and left for dead. I waited for him to speak, but he didn't say a word.

He went into the bathroom for a few minutes, then came out and washed his face and hands and brushed his teeth, just like he normally did when he was ready for bed. When he finished, he came over to the sofa where I sat and took a seat next to me. After a moment of twiddling his fingers, he finally spoke.

"So, are you going to tell me what happened?"

I turned to look at Charles. He'd sat back on the sofa with a concerned look on his face, waiting for me to begin, but I was at a loss for words.

He took a deep breath. "Breanna, were you with Linden?"

"Why would you even think…," I began.

"Right after you saw him, you came up with the bright idea of leaving with your mother and telling me to meet you later on at your grandfather's house, but you never showed up and you didn't even call!" He took another deep breath. "Then I get a "message" to meet you here at the room and when I get here you look as if you've been through some kind of emotional torment or something! So what am I supposed to think?"

"I'm going through something right now and I really needed my mother today. Charles, you have to believe me. I didn't know the evening was going to end up this way."

"Well, right now I'm going through something also and I really need *you*, so I need you to talk to me, Breanna. Please!"

"I'm pregnant," I said silently.

"Pregnant?" Charles' eyes opened wide and he rose from the sofa and sat on the ottoman in front of me.

He took my hands. "Bree, how long have you known?"

"I found out Monday, but the next morning Granny passed away and then I had to come home. Listen, I know that we hadn't planned for this and I understand if…,"

"Understand if what?" he broke in.

"If you aren't ready for this," I finished.

Charles just sat there with his head in his hands. Moments went by.

"Baby, please say *something*. I'm sorry, Charles." I cried.

"Sorry?" Charles lifted his head and tears ran down his face. "Breanna, this is the most beautiful day of my life. You're telling me that you're pregnant with my child? There's no sorrow in that. I'm the happiest man in the world!"

He got down on his knees and laid his head in my lap, while I rubbed his back.

"Marry me, Breanna." He looked up at me. "I've asked you before, but you wanted to wait. Now I'm asking you again. I've never been happier. *You're* the person that I want to share my life *and* grow old with! Will you marry me?"

Tears streamed down my face. The thought of someone loving me so genuinely felt better than I ever dreamed possible.

"Yes! Yes, I will marry you!" I answered.

Charles threw his arms around me. "I love you, baby!"

"I love you, too! But, I'm scared. Everything is happening so fast."

"You don't have to be afraid, Bree. We're in this together and I'm with you every step of the way. Do you trust me?"

I nodded. "Yes, Charles. I trust you."

"I'm gonna be a father!" he shouted.

"So, tell me. How do you feel right now?" he asked.

"Well, to be honest, I'm exhausted," I said. "I know it's early, but I'd really like to lie down."

"You're right. It *has* been a pretty full day and I could use some sleep also."

Charles lifted me from the sofa and carried me over to the bed. The cool, crisp sheets felt good against my skin and Charles felt good all snuggled up behind me with his arm thrown over my waist. I'd never given it a second thought before, but for some reason, his warm breath on the back of my neck felt so reassuring tonight.

The whole day had been quite an ordeal. I buried my grandmother and I was declaring right here and right now, that I'm burying the past. Mama was right. I cannot change what has happened in the past and it's far too hurtful and painful to keep reliving over and over again. But, I did have the power to choose my destiny, and I just learned that confessing that is powerful in itself.

After Charles had fallen asleep I lay awake thinking and imagining the kind of parents we'd be. Would we take walks in the park or Disney vacations? Or how about become active in the PTA at our child's school? I wondered if we'd have a girl or a boy, and what we'd name him or her.

So many thoughts ran through my mind, but my body had just about come to a complete halt from exhaustion. My eyelids were heavy from all the crying I'd done, not to mention the fact that I hadn't had any sleep. For the next twelve hours, I made up for it. Charles and I lay undisturbed in the same position all night. Finally, we were surrounded by peace and calm, with nothing but the hum from the air conditioner, and a hint of the moonlight that peeked in between the opening in the drapes.

TWENTY-SEVEN

I was awakened by sweet whispers in my ear, tender kisses on my face and neck, and the scent of fresh flowers.

I thought I was dreaming.

"Wake up, beautiful," Charles whispered.

When I opened my eyes, he was kneeling on the side of the bed, fully dressed. There were a dozen long-stemmed red roses, beautifully wrapped and tied in a white satin ribbon lying on the bed next to me.

"Oh, my God! Charles! They're beautiful." I propped myself up with a pillow against the headboard.

"Ahhh." I put the roses to my nose and inhaled deeply.

"Where in the world did you find such beautiful flowers so early on a Sunday morning?" I asked.

"Where there's a will, there's a way," he replied. "*And* it pays to be nice to the front desk clerk because you never know *who* he knows."

I chuckled. "I love them," I said as I smelled them again.

"I just want you to know how special you are to me."

"You show me every day, Charles."

I glanced at the clock on the nightstand to see what time it was and noticed a white envelope with my name on it.

"What's that?" I asked, pointing to the envelope.

"Oh, I'm sorry. I was so excited last night that I forgot to give it to you. It's from your grandfather," he said. "He gave one to all of the grandchildren."

I threw back the sheets and reached for the envelope.

It was sealed and had a printed label that read *Breanna Elaine Baker*.

I slowly opened the envelope and pulled out the contents. I had to blink a couple times to make sure that I was seeing things clearly. I couldn't believe my eyes.

"What's wrong, Bree?"

"Nothing! I just don't believe what I'm seeing!" I passed the check to Charles.

"*Twenty Thousand Dollars?*" We looked at each other in amazement.

"Papa said that Granny had recently sold some prime land that was in her family for a long time, and the attorney said the deal was sweet, but this is *much* more than I expected!"

"What will you do with it, Bree?"

"I'm not sure. Maybe save it for our child's future? I'm sure we'll find plenty of good use for it."

I slid the check back into the envelope and put it in my purse for safe keeping.

"Maybe when we get back home we can talk to that investment guy you met. What's his name, baby?" I asked.

"Yes. Baxter McKinney! I hear he's definitely the man to talk to. I'll give him a call when we get back to Atlanta and set something up."

"It's almost eight o'clock. What do you want to do this morning?" I asked

"Well, I'd like *you* to get showered and dressed so that I can take my beautiful wife-to-be out for breakfast. After that, I'm at your mercy," he said. "Do you know a nice place nearby?"

"Let's see. There's Cracker Barrel right off the interstate heading south. We can go there, and after breakfast we can go by Papa's to say good-bye."

"And then stop at your mother's house after that, before heading home?" he added.

"Sounds like a plan to me."

While Charles packed his bags, I decided on an outfit that would be comfortable for the ride home. He offered to press the wrinkles out of it while I took a shower, so I grabbed my toiletry bag and headed into the shower.

When I was alone, I had time to reflect back on what took place at Mama's house yesterday. I never thought in a million years that I would've learned anything as horrible as the secret that my family has hidden all these years. Honestly, I couldn't be angry with *them*. They had so many people to protect and they'd kept this terrible thing between themselves all this time so that we would all have a chance to live normal lives.

For so many years I tried to comprehend why Dee became so detached from everything after the accident. Now I understand. I still don't know the details behind what happened, but I've decided that I didn't need or want to know. It would only bring more pain, and that's something that I was tired of living with. I needed strength and courage to move on.

God, please guide my steps, and please protect everyone that I love.

When I finished showering, Charles was waiting to rub me down with body cream. I was not a fussy person, but I had to admit that I absolutely loved the pampering that I was getting!

We finished packing and checked around the room to make sure that we weren't leaving anything.

"Wait! Do we have my laptop?" I asked as we were leaving the room.

"Got it right here." Charles swung around to show me the case hanging on his shoulder.

While Charles loaded our bags in the car, I checked out at the front desk. The clerk asked if I liked my flowers.

"Yes! As a matter of fact, I love them!" I said.

"If you're ever in town again, my cousin has her own shop and she does special occasions." He winked at me and gave me her business card.

"*Miracles.*" I whispered the business name that was on the card.

"Yes, *Miracles*," the clerk repeated as he handed me the credit card receipt.

I thanked him and slid the business card into my wallet.

"Ready for breakfast?" Charles asked as I slid into the passenger side.

"For some reason, this morning I'm famished," I replied, rubbing my stomach.

"Just hit the interstate heading south and its two exits down."

We enjoyed a hearty, country-style breakfast at Cracker Barrel while we talked about our favorite baby names and the things we'd always dreamed of doing when we became parents. Charles said that he wanted to take lots of family vacations like his family did when he was a child. I looked forward to doing that since I didn't have that luxury growing up. I revealed that I'd always wanted to go to church as a family. I loved going to church with Mama when I was young, but we never did it as a whole family.

Every now and then, my mind wandered away from our conversation and I thought about Dee and Daddy, but I promised myself that I wouldn't let that horrible secret from the past ruin my future.

Charles smiled. "I'd like that, too. Why don't we start looking for a church when we get back home?" he suggested.

I smiled and took another sip of orange juice.

"Honey, it's almost ten-thirty. We'd better head to Papa's house if we're going to get on the road by noon."

Charles took care of the bill and we jumped back onto the interstate headed south to Fort Mill. We arrived at Papa's house to find Aunt Geri, Uncle Bill, and Sonetta in the kitchen with Papa. Aunt Geri was serving up breakfast plates just as we walked through the door.

"We wanted to come by and see everyone before we head back home," I said.

"Y'all pull up a chair and have some breakfast," Papa said. "Geri made enough to feed an army."

Charles rubbed his stomach. "No, thank you. We just had a big breakfast at Cracker Barrel."

"Is Dee on the sun porch?" I asked, headed that way.

"Her favorite place," Papa said.

"I'll be right back, Charles," I said as I walked down the hall toward the back of the house.

"Dee," I said as I opened the door leading to the screened-in area.

Dee was sitting in a rocking chair, looking out over the huge back yard. I took a seat in the empty rocker next to her and placed my hand over hers on the arm rest.

"We had so much fun out there when we were growing up, didn't we?" I paused as I remembered the barbecues and hide-and-seek games. "I miss those days."

She kept rocking.

"I came by to see you before I leave. Charles and I are heading back to Georgia in a little while." I paused again. "Dee, I have good news; I'm going to have a baby."

She squeezed my hand and closed her eyes. Everything in my heart believed that she was happy for me, and relieved to know that I'd found happiness in my life.

I placed her hand to my mouth and kissed it.

"I'll be back soon. I love you, Dee." I wiped a tear that had fallen from my eye and headed back to the kitchen to say good-bye to everyone else.

I hugged Aunt Geri and Uncle Bill. Sonetta rose from the table and hugged me.

"Bye, Breanna. I love you," she said.

"I love you too, Sonetta. Hey, have fun in cheerleading camp and make sure you read all those books on that list!"

"Here, let me walk you to your car," Papa said as he rose from the table.

"I'm sorry about last night, Papa." I grabbed his hand. "I really wanted to be here for the meeting."

"Oh, don't worry about it, baby girl. Your mother explained all about how she couldn't find her medicine and y'all had to go pick up a new prescription."

"Did you open your envelope yet?" he asked.

"Yes, and I was quite surprised. I had no idea it would be so much. Thank you, Papa." I kissed his cheek.

"Oh, it was your grandmother's doing; thank her."

"I will."

Charles cleared his throat. "Mr. Baker. Sir. I want to marry Breanna. I plan to take good care of her, sir, and I would like your blessing."

Papa looked at me, surprised, and immediately saw the sparkle in my eyes. "Yes, of course you can marry my baby girl," he said. "I know you will take care of her."

"Papa, we're going to have a baby."

He reached into his pocket and pulled out a handkerchief and wiped his eyes.

"That's wonderful news, baby girl. It's a *miracle*. I'm so happy for you both."

"Thank you, sir," Charles said as he tried to shake Papa's hand.

"Well I guess you can call me Papa, now," he said happily as he hugged Charles.

I kissed Papa and thanked him for everything.

"I love you," I whispered before we got in the car and backed out of the driveway.

Papa waved as we drove away. "I love you, too, baby girl."

Mama's house was the next stop before heading back to Georgia. I had to go by and tell her everything that transpired after we talked yesterday evening. I knew she'd be happy when she heard the news that Charles and I had to share.

TWENTY-EIGHT

Mama was in the middle of preparing a big Sunday dinner when we arrived. She thought some of the family members who were still in town might come by before leaving, and she always made enough on Sundays for drop-ins and unexpected guests.

We went into the family room where everyone was watching television.

"Hey!" I said. "We're getting ready to head back to Georgia."

"So soon?" Dante said.

"I've been here almost the entire week!"

"Charles, will you excuse me for a few minutes?" I asked. "I'm going to talk to my mother in the kitchen."

Mama was testing a pound cake in the oven to see if it was done.

"Bree!" She sat the oven mitts down. "Are you okay?"

I nodded. "I'm fine, Mama."

We sat down at the kitchen table.

"Listen, baby. I know what you learned last night was a lot to absorb. God knows I prayed that you'd never know." She grabbed my hands. "But now that you do, I'm praying that you'll be able to forgive everyone so that you can move on and be happy."

"I do, Mama. I forgive everyone." I didn't want to cry again, but I couldn't stop the tears from falling.

"I told Charles that I'm pregnant, Mama."

"Oh, thank God! What did he say, Bree?"

"He said that he's the happiest man in the world." I paused. "And he asked me to marry him." I smiled.

"Oh, my God! Bree! Did you accept?"

"Yes. We're getting married."

Mama jumped up from the table and threw her arms around me, crying tears of joy.

"I'm so happy for you, baby," she said. "Charles loves you – I can see it in his eyes."

We walked into the family room holding hands and everyone stopped talking.

"What are you two crying about?" Bliss asked.

She turned to me. "Can I tell them?"

"Go right ahead."

"Breanna and Charles are getting married!"

"Getting *married*?" Bliss repeated the words, looking shocked.

"Congratulations!" Bonita said as she jumped up from her seat to hug us both.

"And there's more," Mama said. "They're having a baby!"

"Oh, my goodness! Bree, congratulations!

"Welcome to the family, Charles," Dante said, shaking his hand.

I was elated to see everyone's excitement about our news, but even more touched to see how they were celebrating the new life that was growing inside me. Just knowing that my family loved me so much, and so unconditionally, touched me deep within, in a place that I didn't even know existed until today. I've never felt closer to them than I did right then.

We told them that Charles wanted to share the good news with his family first, and that we'd call to update them with our wedding plans.

I sighed. "I hate to leave, but we've got to hit the road."

Charles chimed in. "It really was good seeing you all again."

Everyone walked outside to see us off and as we were backing out of the driveway, Mama blew a kiss and mouthed the words, *I love you.*

I waved all the way until Charles turned the corner of the block.

"I know you're going to miss them."

I took a deep breath. "Yes, I am," I said. "But its time to go home."

I directed Charles to I-85, which we'd take all the way back to Atlanta. On the way home we talked about our lives and where we'd go from here. Charles was too excited to wait, so we called his family from the road and shared the news about the baby and our plans to get married. They, too, were overjoyed and asked us to call as soon as we had a date.

I never imagined that this would bring so much joy to other people's lives, but I found out that bringing a baby into the world could mean something much deeper than tradition. To me, it meant that there was something greater than me – something greater than my problems. It meant hope for a brighter future, and I was so thankful for the vision to see beyond just the surface.

TWENTY-NINE

Charles and I decided there was no reason to wait, so we planned to get married right away. We chose to have a small church ceremony next month in my home town with our families and closest friends joining us for the wedding and a formal dinner to follow.

I ordered flowers and arrangements from *Miracles,* and although I'd never met the owner before then, she went above and beyond to put an extra special touch on everything. I guess Charles really struck a heart string with the front desk clerk at the hotel that morning after he learned he was going to be a father.

When I told Camilla the news, she cried. My best friend, who sometimes appeared to have a heart of stone, was suddenly sentimental.

"Bree, I knew when I first laid eyes on Charles that he was the man for you. What made you have a change of heart?"

"Granny," I said.

Was it a coincidence that she passed away just after I'd found out the news about my pregnancy, and was it a coincidence that Attorney Simmons showed me the paper that indicated Sonetta was my sister? Maybe. All I knew was that up until the time that Granny passed away, I just existed. My life had no real purpose or direction. Depression had crept its way into my family many years ago and trickled down in such a way that I didn't even know *I* was living with it. I couldn't fathom the thought of genuine happiness and unconditional love without feeling guilty that other people that I loved didn't have the same. It never dawned on me that Mama might be satisfied with her life just the way it was, and that Dee's world doesn't have to be my world just because we once shared the same womb.

The week that Granny died, I went through some pretty rough valleys, but when I looked back and evaluated all I'd come through, I new that I could go on. I talked myself through the challenges, constantly reminding myself that I am strong.

Just look how far you've come! Now, imagine what you can do when you live with purpose.

I'm learning and growing, but also finding that we sometimes inspire others when we don't even know that they're watching.

A letter came in the mail today, postmarked from Charlotte, North Carolina.

Dear Breanna;

I'm glad that we had the chance to talk when you were home for Granny's funeral. Even though I never told you, I do thank you for being real with me. I've been doing a lot of thinking about what you said and you're right. There are a lot better things I can do with my life than dancing in a club with a bunch of disgusting men grabbing at my crotch. I was trying to go about things the fast and easy way, but in the long run, I found that it's not easier at all.

Anyway, I wanted you to know that I've been researching schools for performing arts. I might even be able to start the fall semester. I can get a college education and become a star at the same time!

Say hello to my brother-in-law for me. Oh, and you'll be glad to know that I put the money that Granny left for me into an account to help with my college tuition if I need it.

Love always,
Bliss

I laughed. She still wants to be a star. *Oh, well. Bliss will always be Bliss.* But I think she's going to be alright.

About the Author

S.D. Denny began writing poetry and short stories at an early age to escape the harsh realities she faced while growing up in a Brooklyn housing project. On her journey to becoming a published author, she has written and edited training material for national organizations and volunteered as a journalist for a church magazine. In addition to her debut novel, *The Baker's Dozen*, she is the author of an erotic anthology, and a contributing author to *The Breakthrough: a Triumph of My Soul Anthology*, with her short story entitled *Shattered Mirrors*. She currently lives in North Carolina. You can visit the author on her website at www.sddenny.com.

The Baker's Dozen

Ordering Information

Yes! Please send me ________ copies of
S.D. Denny's, *The Baker's Dozen.*

Please include $15.00 plus $2.00 shipping/handling for the first book and $1.00 for each additional book.

<u>Send my book(s) to:</u>

Name:_______________________________________
Address:_____________________________________
City, State, Zip:_______________________________
Telephone:___________________________________
Email:_______________________________________

Would you like to receive emails from
Peace In The Storm Publishing?
____Yes ____No

Peace In The Storm Publishing, LLC.
Attn: Book Orders
P.O. Box 1152
Pocono Summit, PA 18346

<u>VISIT US ON THE WEB</u>
www.PeaceInTheStormPublishing.com

Printed in the United States
148789LV00004B/2/P